Los Cuentitos

A Book of Tales

BY ANA ORTIZ

ISHMAEL
TREE

NEW YORK, NEW YORK

THE ISHMAEL TREE
www.ishmaeltree.com

Cover Art: Alyssa Campos

978-1-945959-52-3
eBook: 978-1-945959-53-0

First and foremost, I would like to thank my heavenly Father.

*There are many people who have supported me an encouraged me
on this journey. I want to thank all the persons who read the stories
or who patiently sat and listened to me read the stories:
Solangel Campos, Sonali Ortiz,
Orlando Ortiz, Nestor Ortiz,
Esteban Ortiz, Alyssa Campos, Becky Arias, Nancy Ramos,
Josmely Francisco, all the members of
the Bronx Write Now Circle, and every other unsuspecting person
that would just listen.*

*Special thanks to Richie Narvaez for taking the time to read my
stories and giving me feedback. I am grateful to Gary Axelbank for
publishing my stories in This Is The Bronx Magazine. My heartfelt
appreciation to my publisher Giselle Ishmael who never gave up
on me.*

Thank you for all your hard work.

Ana

Table Of Contents

1. Bitches In Batas

2. Black With No Teeth Rides The Bus

3. Carmencita

4. How My Mother Lost Her Job

5. La Pista (The Arena)

6. Model Double Helix XY

7. Shardonnay Jones Moves In

8. The Day I Almost Died

9. The Night I Met BB Hatchet

10. The Patient In Bed 508 (1)

11. There are Ghosts Living In My House

12. Whatever Happened to El Brujo

CHAPTER ONE

Bitches in Batas

The laundry mat was almost full that early hot summer morning although it was a weekday. It was in the high 100's and hot as hell. All the housewives in the neighborhood would try to get in there by 6:00 am in order to be out before the sweltering heat turned it into a sauna. In the background, you could hear the lyrics of an unrequited love song, *"Amores como el tuyo se encuentran en la calle (Your kind of love can be found in the streets)…"* floating from the radio on the wall.

Luzmar was taking the clothes out of the washer and putting them in the cart. Luzmar was wearing a pink bata (housedress) covered with white lilies and matching hot pink flip flops.

She saw something familiar out of the corner of her eye and when she took a closer look was almost certain that she recognized her man's shirt in the cart next to her. Luzmar had been living with her man Rodolfo for two years now.

Zoraida was standing in front of the washer next to Luzmar. She was lost in thought, daydreaming about what happened the night before when she and Rodolfo made passionate love and he promised his undying love to her. Zoraida could not wait until the day that she and Rodolfo would be together forever. She had been with him for several months now and was waiting for the engagement ring in order to set the wedding date. Zoraida was abruptly awakened from her fantasy when Luzmar screamed,

"I know whose shirt that is...that is my man's shirt!" Zoraida turned to look at Luzmar and replied,

"No, it is not." Luzmar began to sort through the clothes in Zoraida's cart and realized that it was not just Rodolfo's shirt but also his pants and underwear. In fact, all of the clothes in Zoraida's cart belong to Rodolfo. Luzmar said,

"Yes, this is Rodolfo's shirt!"

Zoraida grabbed Luzmar's arm and told her to keep her hands off the clothes. That is how the fight started. Luzmar who was now livid with rage after finding all of her man's clothes in another woman's basket, grabbed Zoraida by her bata and flung her against the washer.

Zoraida wore a blue bata covered with red roses and it was now open exposing most of her thighs and red thongs. In an attempt to be free from Luzmar's hold, Zoraida pushed the cart in front of her with her legs thereby pinning Luzmar against the wall. The people in the laundry mat formed a circle around the two women who were now in the midst of a full blown brawl. They shouted words of encouragement as the women continued to beat each other to a pulp.

10

"Yeah, beat that ho's ass."

"Fuck that home wrecker up..."

It was at this point, that Ahmed, the laundry mat manager came in and separated the two women and broke up the instigating circle of spectators. Both women were badly beaten and bruised.

Zoraida's face was swollen and red from being bashed into the washer and Luzmar had a black eye and several cuts from the assault of the laundry cart. The argument continued in front of the laundry mat where in culminated with a plan.

The two women decided to confront Rodolfo. To his amazement, Rodolfo found both his women waiting for him when he arrived at Luzmar's home that afternoon. Rodolfo recovered quickly from the shock and like every drug user proceeded to lie and manipulate his way out of the situation. Rodolfo told Luzmar,

"You are the love of my life; no other woman could take your place mami."

Zoraida could not believe her ears because these was the very same lines he had used on her.

"Oh my God, you are such a liar!"

"Shut the fuck up, you grimy bitch!"

Luzmar was dumbfounded and did not know who to believe. Rodolfo professed his undying love for Luzmar and told Zoraida to get the hell out of his house. Humiliated and distraught Zoraida left Luzmar's house and went home to nurse her wounds and bruised ego.

• • •

A few days later, while having a few Coronas at The Pitbull Lounge, the local bar, Rodolfo bumped into Zoraida. He apologized profusely,

"But *Bebé*, you know I love you only. I promise I will never do that again."

Rodolfo was so convincing that he managed to negotiate a trip home with Zoraida that night. He quickly passed out after their love making session. At that moment, it all became very clear to Zoraida; she knew exactly what to do. Zoraida quietly slipped away and took Rodolfo's cell phone from his pants. She then dialed Luzmar's phone number and told her,

"If you want Rodolfo, he is right here, come and get him." It was approximately 2 am when Luzmar arrived at the apartment and found the love of her life passed out in Zoraida's bed. Luzmar became so angry; her face was almost as red as the crimson color bata she was wearing when she started screaming Rodolfo's name.

"Rodolfo, you two timing "cabrón (dumb ass), I am going to kill you!"

Rodolfo who was in deep sleep, jumped out of bed, his head nearly missing the ceiling when he heard the unmistakable voice of Luzmar. Even in his drunken and drugged stupor, Rodolfo knew he was in Zoraida's apartment. Luzmar took the broom and started to beat Rodolfo who was naked and holding a bed sheet around his body. Zoraida was laughing uncontrollably at the sight of Rodolfo getting his ass beaten by Luzmar.

He was now wide awake after getting hit several times with the broomstick. In between swings, Rodolfo managed to get a hold of his pants that where on the floor next to the bed and get them on. Zoraida stuck her leg out from underneath her green frilly bata and tripped Rodolfo just as he made a wild dash pants strewn about on the streets,

"Hey bro, peep this."

"What?"

"Mad clothes. Look at this, camo pants and a hoodie."

Jay and Sonny decided to use the clothes to build the headquarters tent for their guerrilla warfare games. Since it was such a beautiful morning, one of the neighbors also decided to use one of the tee shirts to wash his car.

Later that evening, the neighborhood drunk , Pablo, was seen wearing one of Rodolfo's City Jeans shirt. One of the kids snickered,

"Oye Pablo, where you get the dope shirt?"

"You like it? Brand new from City Jeans." The kids broke out in uncontrollable laughter.

•••

About one month later that summer, Rodolfo was seen at the laundry mat waiting in front of dryer for his clothes. In the background you could hear the lyrics of a love betrayed, *"Y si el corazon llora...le pido que se calle...* (And if my heart cries... I ask it to be quiet...), floating from the radio on the wall.

CHAPTER TWO

Black Man With No Teeth Rides the Bus

There were no empty seats on the bus that morning. It was a balmy 23 degrees and everyone standing at the bus stop wanted to obtain passenger status on the BX 55. Despite repeated efforts, Willie was still at the end of the line of the persons boarding and had only managed to make it to the third step inside of the bus.

Maria Elena Santos had only managed to get a seat on the bus because she was the third stop on the route. She was sitting in the second seat to your right as you entered the bus. Maria Elena had to place both hands in front of her because she feared that Willie would have ended up sitting on her lap.

Willie who had consumed a bottle of Wild Turkey for breakfast earlier that morning was standing right behind Estha. She was trying to steady herself between the movement of the bus and the constant pushing on her back. Willie was on his way to Anger Management class as required by the conditions of his probation. Estha, the victim of both spousal and alcohol abuse, was on her way to her daily meeting of Take Your Life Back. Estha looked up only to find that the entire center aisle was totally occupied and there was no room to move. In her hazy mind, Estha was trying to figure out how she could maneuver further along to the back when she heard the argument in the distance. Willie yelled,

"Can't you see there is no more room to move back?!"

The bus driver replied,

"Sir, I will not move until you step behind the white line. Please move to the back of the bus!"

Willie's anger had escalated and his face, now contorted, exposed his gums. He had been a runner for the local crack dealers in his neighborhood in the mid-eighties and had been beaten within an inch of his life on several occasions. It was for this reason and the fact that he too had succumbed to the wiles of Lady C that he had lost most of his teeth.

Estha turned around just as Willie shoved her and said,

"Come on, sista, move!"

She looked at her brother through blood shot eyes but did not respond. Estha had learned a long time ago to say as little as possible to her brother.

"Come on now Estha show these people the bus driver means business!"

Willie then pushed his sister so hard, Estha catapulted to the middle of the aisle amidst the protests of her fellow passengers.

"Hey, Bro, what are you doing?"

"Stop pushing!"

"You almost landed on my lap!"

"What the fuck!"

"I'm going to knock the rest of your teeth out!"

Willie continued to insist that his sister move further back in the bus although there was a human wall of resistance. Willie then said,

"I know why you are doing me this way? You're talking to me like this because I'm Black."

The bus was now approaching the next stop on the route, when it swerved and came to an abrupt halt in an attempt to avoid hitting a bicycle rider that had made a right turn in front of it. At that precise time, Willie pushed his sister towards the back. Estha who had grown weary of her brother's bullying decided to move to the side which resulted in Willie lunging forward, his head hitting Jamal directly on his chest.

Jamal was about 6'5" tall and weighed approximately 225 pounds. A rising basketball star at his local high school, he was on his way to practice that morning and preparing for a very important game coming up where a scout was coming to see him perform.

Jamal felt the searing pain shoot through his chest as though his body had come into contact with a brick wall. His initial response was to defend himself from the unprovoked onslaught. Jamal shot up from the impact of Willie's head on his chest, the pain emanated from a place he did not know existed in his body. With one hand he grabbed Willie's head and with the other he punched him in the mouth thereby loosening the remainder of his teeth. The defensive blow to Willie's rib cage was instinctual and in part caused by the trauma to Jamal's body. Willie became so enraged he reached down and pulled a knife from the side of his boot, a residue from his running days, and swung at Jamal.

Most of the passengers on the bus heard the sirens before they realized that Jamal had been wounded. It was not until they saw the pool of blood form at the bottom of his feet that they grasped the severity of the situation.

The Emergency Services Ambulance arrived but there was very little that the paramedics could do for Jamal, since his aorta had been severed by the boot knife and he had died almost instantly.

It took several officers to subdue Willie while they arrested him who repeatedly yelled,

"I know why you are doing this to me. You're doing this to me 'cause I'm Black!"

CHAPTER THREE

Carmencita

Carmencita met Roberto when she worked as an Assistant Night Manager at the Two Hot Wings, the chicken spot on the block. Roberto had been keeping an eye on Carmencita for awhile now. He was smittened with her beauty. He would often come in during her shift under the pretense of ordering hot wings just to strike up a conversation,

"Hola preciosa (beautiful), how are you doing this evening?"

"Oh, the same old. How about you?"

"Great now that I'm here with you mami chula." Carmencita always blushed and smile at the nightly adoration she received from Roberto.

One evening, he finally got up the courage to invite her out to dinner.

"Preciosa (beautiful), you think you might like to go out to dinner with me on your night off?"

Carmencita agreed to go to dinner with Roberto at Joe's Place. They met there one Sunday evening as planned, and enjoyed the excellent Puerto Rican Cuisine and several glasses of white wine while getting to know one another. Carmencita asked Roberto,

"What do you do when you are not eating hot wings?'

Roberto laughed. He was six feet tall, had light brown hair, and coffee colored eyes that twinkled whenever he smiled.

"I am studying architecture."

"Wow, I did not see that coming..."

He was intelligent, incredibly charming but rather impulsive. It was this impulsiveness that would often get him into more scrapes than he could count or get out of. However, it was Roberto's intelligence that won him a scholarship to one of those prestigious universities that people read about but never get to experience.

"I am going to design the first storm resistant dome house in Buena Vista."

"Well, that is pretty ambitious!" Roberto winked and smiled at Carmencita.

"I am an ambitious type of guy, nothing but the best for me."

"It is a great idea since Puerto Rico is always plagued by hurricanes."

"Enough about me. What do you do when you are not working at the Two Hot Wings?"

"I work at night because I attend a program during the day. I am in training to become a Financial Analyst."

"That is amazing. Not too many Puerto Rican women study Finance. You must come from a smart family."

Carmencita's eyes darkened and her smile faded. Carmencita was olive skin with black raven hair and midnight blue eyes. She was the child of an inter racial one night stand between a Puerto Rican mother and Italian father. Her mother, Socorro spent the remaining years of her life pining for a man she could never have. The pain was so unbearable that she succumbed to drugs. Carmencita said,

"Oh no, it's just my life has not been easy. But I suppose no one life's is ever easy."

"What do you mean?"

Carmencita was first taken from her drug addicted mother at the age of seven. Socorro would go to rehabilitation and recover for periods of time. Carmencita was reunited with her mother on several occasions but never for very long. She was present when they took her mother away in a body bag because she had overdosed. There was no money for a funeral and no relatives around to help. Carmencita was taken directly to a youth home because she was too old for foster care or adoption. Carmencita explained,

"I grew up mostly in foster care and then in a youth home."

At the youth home, Carmencita was recruited by the project "*Alas Para Volar*" (Wings To Soar). The goal of the project was to to groom under privileged but gifted young persons for entry level positions in major corporations. Roberto always knew the right thing to say,

"Yes, but those experiences have made you into the strong, intelligent, and beautiful woman you are today."

It was on this night that began their doomed relationship.

· · ·

Roberto and Carmencita continued to go out and their relationship grew over the next few months. They fell madly in love with one another and began to make plans for their future together. Roberto told Carmencita,

"I want you to meet my family. My mother is going to love you!"

Because of her history, Carmencita was nervous about meeting his family. *"What if his mother does not think I am good enough for her son."* Despite her misgivings, she agreed to meet his mother and brother. Roberto was so happy that he immediately brought Carmencita home to meet his small family, his mother Monse and younger brother Joselito. They too quickly became enamored with her. Just as expected, Monse was ecstatic,

"Hay pero que bella! (Oh, how beautiful!) At last, I get to have the daughter I always prayed for. What a blessing!"

Carmencita moved into the Santiago home and soon became a permanent member of the household. Roberto suggested that they postpone the wedding until after graduation. Carmencita thought this was best for both of them. They began their preparations.

"You can get a job with that big pharmaceutical company in Buena Vista."

"That is an excellent idea. You can work on the plans to build our dream house."

Thus, began their life together, full of so much promise and hope for the future.

· · ·

One night while working at the Two Hot Wings, Carmencita became nauseous. When she came out of the bathroom, her co-worker Luzmar asked her,

"Girl what is wrong with you? You look *hincha* (pale), like you saw a spirit or something."

"I dunno, but it feels like I've just thrown up my *tripas* (guts).

"You should go home if you don't feel good. This stupid job ain't worth it!"

Luzmar had started working part time at the Two Hot Wings in order to make some extra cash after she threw out that two timing *cabrón* (dumb ass). Carmencita went home early that night and passed out.

It was not until early morning that she realized her menstruation was late. The clock ticked slowly and nine a.m. could not come fast enough. Carmencita telephoned the doctor's office and spoke to the receptionist about scheduling an appointment for a pregnancy test.

"Hi Mildred, this Carmencita. I want to schedule an appointment for a pregnancy test?"

"When was your last period?"

After some quick calculations, Mildred suggested that Carmencita should come on down that morning for the test. At approximately three in the afternoon, she received the news that she was pregnant. Carmencita could not wait to tell Roberto.

Roberto was elated that he was going to be a father and looked forward to the day when the baby would call him *papi*. The rest of the family was delighted with the good news. Monse was so happy that there would soon be a new addition, she began preparations for the baby's nursery. She emptied the back room and hired a contractor to begin remodeling immediately. There was a small alcove located to the right hand side of the room where Carmencita could lie down to take care of the baby. It was decided that Joselito, Roberto's younger brother, would paint the alcove a lovely shade of teal.

. . .

Joselito was a couple of years younger than Roberto, a few inches shorter, and darker. He also had a more muscular body from the endless hours of working out at the gym. Unlike Roberto, Joselito was always running the streets and getting into trouble. When his brother brought Carmencita home, Joselito secretly fell in love with her. Unbeknownst to Roberto, his younger brother had become obsessed with his bride-to-be. Joselito spent many hours fantasizing about Carmencita and raising the baby together.

After Joselito finished painting the room, he called to Carmencita to come take a look. Carmencita was very pleased,

"Oh my God, Joselito, it's so beautiful! Thank you so much."

It was at this moment that he decided to profess his love for Carmencita,

"Carmencita, I love you. I know by the way you look at me that you feel the same."

Carmencita was dumbfounded. Her mouth opened, but no words came out.

"Please marry me. We could raise the baby and have a very happy life together."

Carmencita was in a total state of shock,

26

"Are you crazy?! No, I will not marry you! You must be insane! I am in love with your brother and having his baby."

Joselito pleaded,

"Please don't do this, you know we belong together. We always have!"

Carmencita was now trembling,

"Absolutely not! I belong with Roberto!"

Joselito, who was one short of a six pack, became enraged and pushed Carmencita and she fell to the floor. This was not how Joselito thought it would be. In his delirium, Joselito beat Carmencita. She fought back but did not stand a chance against his brute force.

. . .

Roberto was the one who found Carmencita's lifeless body laying in a pool of blood on the floor of the room adjacent to the nursery. Roberto, horrified by the scene before his eyes, began to sob uncontrollably. He held Carmencita in his arms and rocked back and forth for several hours.

"Mi pobre bebe (my poor baby.) Who could have done something like this?"

Soon Roberto's grief turned into anger, he lost all rationality and the only thing he wanted was retribution. Roberto was determined to find the person who had killed his woman and unborn child.

"I am going to kill the motherfucker when I find him."

He was exiting the building when he bumped into Camacho, Joselito's boy, who was standing at the front entrance. Camacho grabbed Roberto by the arm and begged him,

"Please forgive your brother, he has lost his mind. He doesn't know what he is doing."

The realization that it was his brother who had killed Carmencita sent Roberto over the edge, it was all too much for him to bear. Roberto hunted for his brother until he found him later that evening at the Pitbull Lounge. He shot Joselito, who was drinking a medalla at the bar, in front of at least twenty witnesses.

. . .

The next day, a distraught Monse watched as her eldest son, Roberto was taken away in handcuffs for the murder of her youngest son, Joselito. Monse was numbed from the pain of everything that had happened in the past twenty-four hours. All she wanted was to put an end to the agony. A few hours after the arrest, she climbed unto the chair and managed to put her head in the noose that was hanging over head.

CHAPTER FOUR

How My Mother Lost Her Job

Lucinda Santos was the account manager for the International Money Transfer Office. Her desk was located directly across from her administrative assistant, Shane Santiago.

"Good morning, Ms. Santiago. Have you prayed this morning and asked God to forgive you for your sins?"

Shane dreaded coming to work because Lucinda was a Christian determined to save Shane's soul. Every morning, Lucinda would quote scripture to her. For example, Lucinda would quote Leviticus 20:13: *"If a man lies with a male as with a woman, both of them have committed an abomination."*

"With all due respect," Shane would reply, "my personal business is none of your concern and should not be a topic in the workplace."

"In the Bible," Lucinda persisted, "Paul describes both lesbian and male homosexual behavior as unnatural. Our distorted desires are a sign that we have turned away from God. You must repent and ask for God's forgiveness."

This was the routine every morning for every day of the work week.

. . .

Unbeknownst to Shane, several months earlier, Lucinda had walked into her bedroom to find her 22-year-old son, Gabriel Angel Santos, wearing her clothes and high-heeled shoes.

"What do you think you are doing?!" she screamed, feeling shocked and confused. She was so infuriated that she threw her son out of the apartment and her clothes and shoes into the garbage.

. . .

One Friday morning, when Shane arrived at work, something was different. Instead of receiving the usual greeting, she found Lucinda crying at her desk. Shane did not make any inquiries, but this did not prevent Lucinda from sharing the cause of her affliction. Lucinda said,

"A woman called my home last night to tell me my husband was asleep on her sofa. She wanted to know if I would go to pick him up."

Shane was speechless. Between uncontrollable sobs, Lucinda continued her story.

"I told her that if he was asleep on her couch, then apparently, he was more comfortable in her apartment than in my home, and he should stay there."

Lucinda's husband had been having a relationship with the woman for over six months, and Lucinda had been totally clueless. Finally, Shane found her voice.

"Where is your God now?" she asked.

Enraged, Lucinda jumped over the desk, grabbed Shane by the hair, and bashed her head against the desk repeatedly. Upon entering the office, a customer immediately called the police and attempted to separate the two women.

Lucinda Santos was arrested for assault with intent to cause bodily harm. After being processed at central booking, she called her home and left a message for her daughters. Melinda and Marilu were both home when the call came in, but they did not pick up the phone. They had long ago grown weary of their mother's fanatical religious rantings and wanted nothing to do with her. Gabriel, who had just happened to stop by the apartment, overheard the message when he entered the living room,

"What is wrong with you two? he asked. "Don't tell me that you are planning to leave Mami in jail?"

"We don't even have the money to post bail," Marilu said. "What do you want me to do?"

"I will take care of the bail money. We are not going to let our mother rot in jail."

. . .

Gabriel was a street hustler and used to turning tricks in order to survive. He walked 17th Street and Eighth Avenue nightly as *Gabriela*. Gabriela, a 5'10" statuesque figure with long chestnut hair and dark eyes, used her long beautiful legs to strut her stuff and raise the money in one week.

Every day, Lucinda called her home, but no one picked up. As the days passed, she became more anxious, thinking to herself, *Oh my God, is no one coming to get me out of here?*

The Thursday following her mother's arrest, Gabriela walked into the courtroom with $10,000 in her purse to post bail for her mother Lucinda. A guard came to Lucinda's cell to tell her.

"Hey, Santos, today is your lucky day," said the guard, "your daughter is here to pick you up."

Gabriela was eagerly waiting for her mother. When Lucinda walked into the courtroom, she froze. She could not believe her eyes. Her son was standing there dressed in women's clothing. Lucinda quickly turned on her heels and told the guard,

"That is not my daughter, please take me back to my cell."

Tears rolled down Gabriela's face as she watched the guard escort her mother back to her cell.

CHAPTER FIVE

La Pista (The Arena)

The Velazquez Hacienda had been built at the turn of the 19th century by Victor Manuel's great grandfather. In 1899, the Velazquez Hacienda had become one of the most successful haciendas in the area. The hacienda flourished during this time and the Velazquez family was one of the most respected and feared families in the region. By the 1950's agriculture had declined and the Velazquez family, as well as the displaced farm workers, had to find a new source of income.

The affluence of the Velazquez family diminished as time passed but not its force. The market brought operations at the Hacienda to a standstill by 1955, and, gradually, Hacienda Velazquez fell into disrepair and was partially abandoned until Victor Manuel (the great-grandson of the hacienda's founder) formulated the plan that was to become "La Pista" (The Arena).

And so when almost all of the haciendas had but just about disappeared, the Velazquez family remained one of the most powerful and respected families in the region. Very little was ever discussed about the source of the family's wealth. However, everyone not only knew where the money came from but the fear as well. The families who lived in the area were destitute and did not have many options available to them. It was this poverty that gave birth to and nurtured the arena. La Pista had become one of the viable sources of income for most of the men living in the town of Buena Vista.

Carlos was the youngest of the five Santiago brothers (Arturo, Ramiro, Bernardo, Raul, and Carlos). The Santiago Family had lived in the mountains for over century and was one of the countless casualties of the economic devastation in the area. Carlos' father Don Alvaro had worked for the Velazquez Hacienda as had his grandfather before him. The brothers almost always worked together and looked out for one another. There existed among them a strong family loyalty and unity. But times had changed and all of the Santiago men were now unemployed and only eked out a meager existence by doing odd jobs and some seasonal construction work when it became available.

Every morning Sra. Maria Luisa Santiago prepared breakfast for her family which consisted of six plates of oatmeal lined up on the counter one after the other, a thermos of café con leche already sweetened to taste, and some times bread with butter. Maria made sure that her men had at least one hot meal because she never knew if they would eat again during the day.

Every morning, Doña Maria called out to her boys,

"Come down, breakfast is ready."

The men would start drifting into the kitchen at exactly 7:00 a.m. They would all take their seats at the long counter, after taking their plates of oatmeal. The thermos of 'cafe con leche' would be passed around. This would be their only meal of the day unless they found work. All of them talking at the same time about where they might get an odd job.

"Don Pepe needs a couple of hands to help him with cement work."

"Energía Eléctrica needs men to replace the cables that fell down during the last storm."

"Plaza Del Mercado is looking for delivery men."

Everyone would then go out looking for work.

. . .

One evening while Carlos was drinking a couple of India's with his friends, the conversation turned to the topic of the arena. This had been their daily routine since they had become of legal age to drink the year before. Fernando was discussing how much money they could all make if they registered for "La Pista."

"Oye mano, my older brother Pito won the pot one night at the Pista and all he did was fight one guy."

Fernando loved to brag about how his brother had won the $25,000 pot.

"We can make a lot of money, $100,000 , the four of us in just one night."

Carlos never paid much attention to his friend's endless chatter and self proclaimed expertise on the subject. It was not the first time, the discussion of the arena had taken place at their nightly meetings but there was something different about this evening. One might say that it was the combination of hopelessness and sheer desperation. So that night as the friends sat around and continued to drink beer, the idea of participating in that month's event became a reality.

The first real obstacle to consider was how to raise the money for the entrance fee since only two of them were currently employed and the other two worked sporadically or not at all. Marcos raised the question,

"Where are we going to get the money to pay the entrance fee?" Fernando replied,

"We are going to save every penny until we raise the money. Even if it means we have to stop drinking."

Unbeknownst to Fernando, there was no way that all four of them could enter the arena and each win the price of $25,000. The following morning Fernando spoke to his brother and learned all of the details of participation in the fight.

"It costs a thousand dollars to fight and you have to give your name to Victor Manuel's bodyguard, Chino. He let's you know where the fight is gonna be."

Pito forgot to mention one small detail,that is he never fought in the arena. Although everyone who had lived in Buena Vista had heard of the arena, the Pista's exact location was a total mystery even to those who had lived in those mountains their whole lives. The stories and rumors surrounding the fights were endless but the truth of the matter was that the men who entered the Pista had to pay a fee of a thousand dollars for the privilege of participating in this event. These fees were then deposited into a pot of which $25,000 was awarded to the victor of the fight.

. . .

It took the the group of friends several months to raise the money for only one to enter the match; since there was no way they were able to get enough money together for all four to participate in the event. Now the question was how to choose the person that would represent the group. The friends had consumed several cases of India and were totally inebriated on the night the decision was made. Marcos said,

"The only fair thing to do is to have a drawing."

Elias chimed in,

"Why don't we roll the dice?"

It was decided that they would rolled the dice and the one with the lowest number would be the one to enter *La Pista*. Fernando, who swore he knew everything there was to know about the arena, wanted to go first and rolled a double six. Marcos then rolled a nine. Elias followed closely and rolled an eight. It was Carlos who rolled the lucky seven and was thereby chosen to enter the event. And so it came to pass that Carlos' fate was sealed that night by the roll of the dice.

A week before the scheduled event, the line began to form before sunrise outside of the Velazquez House because everyone wanted to make sure they were able to register before the cut off. After all, the arena could only hold about one hundred men. The arena itself was in the shape of an oval and measured approximately 1875 square feet, it could hold up to 75 persons standing comfortably, so that 100 was already a bit cramped. Carlos and his friends arrived at 4:00 AM thinking that he would the first on line. However, by the time they arrived there were already several men already lined up outside the red door of what was formerly a storage building located on the estate.

"Mira mano (look bro), there are seven already there!"

The actual registration was rather uncomplicated. Chino, one of the men employed by the Velazquez Hacienda, stood at the door took the money and wrote down the name of the prospective combatant in a ledger. On the night of the match, these very same men would line up outside the red door and their names would be checked off the list in much the same manner. Chino motioned for Carlos to come over.

"What are you waiting for? Get over here."

Carlos hesitated as he approached the door and handed the money to Chino with trembling hands.

"What is your name?"

Carlos Jesus Santiago was the seventh name on the list in the ledger. He received the date, time and location of the scheduled fight. Chino instructed further that under no circumstances was he to disclose this information if he wanted to live. Registration went smoothly and was over by 6:00 a.m.

. . .

Carlos and his friends arrived promptly at the scheduled time and place. He approached the red door and gave his name, However, Velazquez's henchmen were quick to stop his three friends.

"Your names are not on the list, you cannot come in."

There was an air of carnival like festivities in and around the Hacienda. It was as if though the smell of blood drew out the animal instinct in all. Upon entering the arena, several weapons were made available to the men. They were given a choice hammers, machetes, and sticks and forced to fight to the death in a gladiator like fashion.

Approximately 100 men could register to enter the Pista at any given event which was held once a month at an undisclosed location. The monthly match developed into a major blood sport where spectators could also paid a fee of a thousand dollars for the privilege of attending the show. Needless to say, the entire event was illegal and violated countless of Buena Vista's laws and ordinances.

Once inside, Carlos and the rest of the men were escorted down a long hallway to the back where they would be held until it was time to enter the arena. The participants would all enter the arena at the same time, at the sound of a gong, through a door that was located at the back of the room where they had been held. Upon entering "La Pista" the weapons were handed to the men and the gates were electronically shut. There were no referees in the arena, only the men, their weapons and the prospect of winning the $25,000. There was no turning back and the only way to leave *La Pista* was to be the last man standing.

The spectators entered through a side door leading inside to the seating in the arena. While waiting for the event to begin, the onlookers were placing side bets on the winner of match. The intensity of the night was so strong it had everyone on the edge of their seats. Carlos broke into a cold sweat with the sudden realization that this match was much more than a fight; his heart was pounding so hard, he could not hear the roar of the crowds sitting in the stands.

Dios mio en que me a metido yo? (Oh my God, what have I gotten myself into?)

Although fighting was a way of life in the mountains and he had won many of the brawls, there was no way that Carlos could ever have prepared for what he would encounter that night. Carlos had never known fear like this and it was that very panic that propelled him into action. The sound of the gong and he chose a machete. Within seconds they were in the ring, the action began and the men entered into combat.

The strong over powering the weak instantaneously, the ravenous devouring the feeble without mercy. Carlos' self preservation instinct kicked in as he began to swing his machete in order to survive. And so the night and carnage progressed, the spectators drinking and cheering on their fighters, hoping to leave a few dollars richer than when they first arrived. Carlos was one of the seven men left among the lifeless bodies and limbs strewn about when three men came up behind, over powering, and throwing him down to the ground. It took two men to pin him down while the third one slit his throat open. His lifeless body dropping to the ground, a large pool of blood formed around his head in the shape of a halo.

. . .

Fernando, Marcos and Elias were lingering outside the red door waiting for their friend to come out. It was the deafening clamor of the crowds inside that signaled the end of the event. They waited anxiously as the hoards of people left the Arena but their friend was nowhere to be seen. Elias was the first to make the observation that none of the participants they had seen the morning of registration and earlier that evening at the entrance of the event were exiting the arena.

"Where are all the fighters? I don't see any of them coming out."

Fernando said,

"Maybe they are all still in the back. Mano no seas tan desperado. (Bro don't be so impatient.)"

44

Marcos reassured his friends,

"Don't worry Carlitos will be coming out soon."

A feeling of dread overcame the group when they saw the last person depart and the red door slammed shut.

. . .

The morning after an event was normally very quiet in the neighborhood. It was as if though the town was already mourning the death of those who had perished the night before in the arena. Sra. Maria Luisa Santiago prepared the customary breakfast for her husband and five sons. The men would started drifting into the kitchen at exactly 7:00 a.m. one after another until they were all seated at the counter in front of their respective plates. Don Alvaro read his paper while the brothers made plans to get work for the day. The minutes passed when Maria noticed Carlos' absence from the counter and started to call out for him,

"Carlitos, you sleepy head, get up and come have breakfast before it gets cold."

When he did not respond, Raul, the one closest to Carlos, when upstairs to check on his younger brother. He yelled out,

"Oye, "manganzón" (Listen you lazy boy) get up already. We are going to be late."

Raul came back downstairs and told his family that Carlos was not in his room and it looked like he had never slept in his bed the night before. Maria Luisa began crying,

"Le a pasado algo a mi bebe. El nunca hace esto. (Something has happened to my baby. He never does this.)"

Arturo told his mother,

"Mama don't worry, I will find him."

The brothers started the search for Carlos by going to the homes of Fernando, Marcos and Elias. Fernando and Marcos were nowhere to be found since they were all too familiar with Arturo's temper and had often been the target of his rage while growing up. When they got to Elias' house, Arturo knocked on the door,

"Elias come out now, we need to talk to you."

It was Elias who had the strength to face the Santiago brothers.

"When did you last see and speak to Carlitos?" Elias apprehensively responded,

"I saw him last night." Arturo looked at him suspiciously,

"Okay, deja la mierda, (cut the shit out) and tell me what happened last night."

"Okay, I saw Carlitos last night at the arena."

Arturo was horrified,

"What the hell?"

"Arturo, please let me explain."

Elias disclosed all the details of their ill fated plan to secure the $25.000. Consumed with grief and rage, the brothers had no idea how to tell their parents that their youngest son who had just turned 21 was dead.

. . .

Arturo assumed his role as the eldest and delivered the news when they arrived home. There was no easy way to tell his parents about his younger brother's death.

"Papa, Mama, I have bad news. Carlitos was killed last night in the arena."

Don Alvaro went numb and did not speak. Maria Luisa became hysterical and started screaming. It took Arturo several hours to get his mother to calm down.

The parents devastated by the news decided that Don Alvaro, who had worked at the Velazquez Hacienda briefly during the 1950's, would personally speak with Luis Manuel to claim their son's body. Don Alvaro arrived early the next morning and requested to speak with Luis Manuel.

"Don Alvaro, its been many years since I've seen you. What can I do to help you?"

Don Alvaro was a mild manner man whose upbringing had taught him to be humble. Particularly with authority.

"Señor Victor Manuel, I came to ask for my son's body."

"What son Alvaro? I have no idea what you are talking about."

"Por favor Señor, my youngest son Carlos Jesus Santiago. He died last night in your Pista."

"I do not know a Carlos Jesus Santiago. And, I definitely do not own a Pista." Don Alvaro lost all composure,

"*Sin sin vergüenza* (without shame), you are going to sit there and lie to my face. Your father must be turning in his grave. Everyone knows you have turned his Hacienda into a slaughterhouse. You should be ashamed of yourself, descarado (shameless)!"

"Chino throw this *viejo pendejo* (old fool) out of here. He lost his marbles and doesn't know what the hell he is talking about."

. . .

Arturo's rage was only fueled further by Victor Manuel's cursory dismissal of his beloved father. I'm going to kill that motherfucker. The Santiago family could not have a proper burial for Carlos because they were unable to recover his body. Nevertheless, the Santiago family held a memorial service for Carlos and mourned his death the customary period of time.

Shortly after, the Santiago brothers decided to avenge Carlos' death. They believed the plan would be easy to execute because no one had ever challenged the Velazquez Family who enjoyed a false sense of security. Don Alvaro was able to provide key information about the physical layout of the Hacienda.

"There are men posted at the front and back entrances of the house. As well as several men in the security office of the Hacienda watching the monitors of the surveillance cameras placed throughout the estate." Ramiro said,

"Yeah, that *hijo de puta* (motherfucker) has a lot men protecting his property." Don Alvaro added,

"The main house also has a garden surrounded by a wrought iron fence. The formal entrance to the Hacienda is through that gate. The day I went to speak Luis Manuel, his man escorted me through the garden."

Raul suggested,

"I don't think that there will be that many men at the Hacienda the day after the match. His men will be too busy." Arturo grew confident,

"Bro, that is an excellent idea."

The discussions and planning would continue for one year until the night finally arrived.

. . .

The night after a match, security at the hacienda was laxed because all the employees were busy cleaning up the mess and disposing of the bodies. The bodies were taken and then buried at a clandestine mass grave site located near an abandoned mill. On this night there was only one man stationed at the main gate in front of the main house.

Victor Manuel together with Macho his right-hand man were sitting at his desk in the study located on the second floor of the main house. The second floor contained three bedrooms and a study located on right at the top of the stairs. Victor Manuel was counting the earnings of the previous night.

When Arturo and his three brothers arrived at the entrance quickly over powered the lone man at the gate and just as easily gained access to the main house. Victor Manuel was the first to hear the footsteps downstairs and dispatched Macho to investigate. As he was descending the stairs, one the brothers fired a shot gun directly at Macho's head. Because of the close proximity of the shot, the pellets contained in the cartridge had not had time to spread, and they entered the body in a single mass, thereby causing the pieces of Macho's skull and brain tissue to be splattered all over the walls and stairs.

Victor Manuel had been hurriedly trying to put the money in the safe, when the brothers came in through the door and assaulted him.

Arturo beat Victor Manuel within an inch of his life and he was barely breathing when they hung him upside from a Ceiba tree located several feet in front of the wrought iron fence surrounding the hacienda.

During the early morning hours, the Buena Vista Fire Department arrived to the piles of ashes that had once been the Velazquez Hacienda. As the patrol car approached the estate, they saw the dangling body from a distance.

When the officers approached the site they found Victor Manuel's limp hanging body and his genitals at the foot of tree.

CHAPTER SIX

Model Double Helix XY

The Life Never Ends facility overlooked the North East River in New City. The river that fifty years ago had been polluted with human and chemical waste was now a clear blue, owing to its treatment with special cleansing agents. Still, it was not safe for consumption. The vast complex consisted of several white and silver IS-shaped buildings. The facility was accessible by train tubes or air. The train tubes were silver and shiny. You could see them in the skyline; their reflection making rainbow colors in the surrounding area.

Both train arrival and departure announcements were transmitted on the telescreens located on the walls throughout the terminal.

"All trains departing lower level."

The candidates attending this facility arrived via these train tubes once a month.

"This train services only the Life Never Ends facility."

In addition to arrivals and departures, the telescreens made public service announcements.

"Report all suspicious activity to the Department of Safety. There are safety dispatchers available twenty-four hours a day to assist you."

The public service announcements were issued by the New City General Assembly.

Raul Santiago waited for the train tube that would take him to the facility. The New City Department of Safety Enforcement officers were discreetly sitting to the left and right of him. Raul had evaded the officers now for over thirty years; he was one of the few humans left in New City.

To any observer, Raul appeared to be just another passenger riding the tubes of New City. He dozed off to the soft humming sound of the tubes, thinking about the previous night. He had been on the floor with Alexandra. They were in one of the many abandoned buildings in the city.

"Wake up, wake up, sleepyhead," Alex said playfully, but Raul would not budge. Alex was wide awake, and as soon as the first sun rays came through the cracks of the boarded windows, she wanted to leave. Alex was feeling hunger pangs because she had not eaten in forty-eight hours. She got bored with Raul and decided to go search for something to eat. Although most of the city's population had no need for nourishment, New City had a strict rationing program to control the food supply, and people like Alex were forced to scavenge for food.

Raul and Alex had grown up and spent many hours playing together in the callejón because not many children were left in the neighborhood. Raul kept a close eye on Alex throughout their childhood and youth. One evening, while Alex worked as night manager for Two Hot Wings, the chicken spot on the block, he finally got up the courage to invite Alex to hang out with him at Pitbull Lounge just around the corner.

"Alex, why don't you hang out with me tonight at the lounge?"

She hesitated. "I don't know about that, Raul. I don't want to ruin our friendship."

After some persuasion, Alex agreed. They met as planned and danced all night to the pulsating beats of the songs playing at the club. Several Medallas and dances later, Raul and Alex decided to go back to her place, where they stayed until the early morning hours while the birds serenaded their lovemaking.

Raul woke up from a deep sleep to the sound of the siren announcing curfew.

His heart beat rapidly as he realized Alex was gone. How many times had he told her not to go out without him or, at the very least, tell him where she was going. He quickly dressed and left in search of her.

Raul reached the corner of Thompson and East 9th Street. Where once a park stood was now a 32-foot-deep crater; the exact location where Raul had picked up Alex two nights ago.

. . .

"Where are you, Alex?"

"I'm near the mainframes in the control room... getting ready to attach the device now."

"Be careful. Let me know when you are near the rendezvous point."

Her heart was pounding, and the adrenaline pumped through her veins. This is what Alex lived for. She set the timer and raced down the stairs and through the underground tunnels. Countless maneuver exercises had prepared her for this moment. She had chosen to train in demolition and explosives. The preparation had often been slow, methodical, and boring. Raul was waiting for her at the end of the underground tunnel.

"Hurry, we have two minutes to get out of here." The back door of the black jeep flung open.

"Hurry, hurry. We're running out of time."

Alex jumped in. Raul sped through the back alleys, swerving and weaving as he dodged every hole and crevice of his second home. As they sped along, Raul watched the building disappear from the skyline in his rear view mirror. Alex saw Raul's lips moving:

"This was a big a score for our side...," but she could only hear the ringing in her ears after the explosion.

"...We have now taken out most the city's key facilities with the exception of Life Never Ends."

A loud beeping noise announcing an incoming transmission for Team Phoenix interrupted the one-sided conversation. A face appeared on the screen of the monitor located on the jeep's dashboard.

"Great job! Please proceed to your designated retrieval point, where you will be transported back to home base to await further instructions for your next target."

The end of the transmission was followed by yet another beep. They would never know the person who gave the orders over the monitor.

Raul and Alex belonged to a group known as Freedom Now, which was opposed to New City's oppressive laws, regulations, and practices. Unbeknownst to Raul and Alex, they had been designated as the next targets because of their skills and experience but, more importantly, their efficiency as a team. The jeep pulled onto a ramp located underneath the abandoned building that had once served as an indoor parking lot. Raul quickly parked the vehicle, and then he and Alex walked through an underground tunnel to an adjacent building that was their temporary shelter. Both of them were exhausted and they passed out as soon as they lay down on the floor.

. . .

Alex had been apprehended shortly after she had left Raul asleep at the retrieval point. Alex was leaving one of the food distribution centers located throughout New City when she spotted the gray jackets as she came around the corner of West 117th and Morningside Park. Her eyes darted around looking for an escape route, but it was too late. She had been blindsided by her hunger.

"Stop, or we shall be forced to terminate you."

They surrounded and arrested Alex for violation of New City's Section 1551: Willful Destruction of Government Property. Alex was immediately taken to a holding facility, where she would be questioned. The New City Department of Safety Enforcement had been looking for Freedom Now members since it had first come to power fifty years ago. It had been unsuccessful in apprehending certain key members who were responsible for the destruction of government property.

Section 1551 protected "any property" of New City or an agency or department thereof, or any property being manufactured or constructed for New City or an agency or department thereof, from willful destruction or attempted destruction. The penalties for violations of this section were imprisonment or death.

Raul and Alex had earned the dubious distinction of being on the city's Top Ten Most Wanted list. The government officials were beside themselves when they finally captured Alexandra Altagracia.

The interrogation room they took her to was 8 by 10 feet, large enough for three individuals to sit comfortably. She was tied to a stainless-steel bench bolted to the floor in the center of the room.

On the right-hand side of the entrance to the room was a silver metal box that controlled the electrical charges that were transmitted to the wires attached to the bench. One of the New City Department of Safety Enforcement Officers was sitting outside looking into the room through a small glass window in the middle of the door. He pushed the button that administered the shocks.

"Just answer the question."

"I don't know the answer. Please stop."

No one could hear Alex's agonizing screams because they were in the bowels of one of New City's two remaining buildings, the Department of Safety Enforcement. The officer increased the voltage.

"Who is in charge of your unit?"

Alex screamed, "I DON'T KNOW!"

"Just answer the question."

"I told you, I don't know. I'm just a soldier."

Alex had been in the room for three days. They would turn on the lights so bright, they would blind her. Then, they would leave her in absolute darkness for hours at a time. The room had no windows, and the temperature was controlled by the silver metal box as well.

Once again, the officer increased the voltage, the room was stifling hot when Alex passed out. On the right wall of the room, the camera recording the interrogation was surreptitiously placed behind a two-way mirror, at a height of about 6 feet, to capture the interrogation in its entirety. Another New City Department of Safety Enforcement Officer was sitting behind the recording device. He came rushing into the room, untied Alex, and tried to revive her. Alex came to long enough to swallow a tiny strip taped to the underside of her breast. Within seconds, she had stopped breathing. By the time the medics arrived, she was already dead.

· · ·

Raul drove through the backstreets of New City desperately searching for Alex. He knew he was taking a big risk being out in the open, but he needed to find her. Their instructions were very clear: go to the point of retrieval and wait for extraction.

Why didn't she wait? he thought to himself.

The Freedom Now organization had many training centers in old abandoned warehouses, factories, and lofts scattered throughout the city. Raul looked in every place she might be, to no avail. His mind was racing from thought to thought. *Where could she possibly be?*

Alex had never deviated from the plan. Raul's instincts told him there was something wrong; she would not have stayed away this long. He was staring into the gaping hole of the crater as though it could provide him with answers when two pairs of arms suddenly reached out from behind Raul and grabbed him, while a third pair injected him with something. He was instantly immobilized and fell to the ground.

Raul awoke in an interrogation room similar to the one in which Alex had been questioned. His hands and feet were cuffed to the steel bench. The room was a chilly 10 degrees, and he was wearing nothing but a T-shirt and pants. In the distance, he could hear a voice speaking but could not make out the words. He could not see anything because it was pitch black. Raul's mind was still hazy from the drug-induced coma, and it took him awhile to get his bearings.

Several hours later, a giant screen appeared on the wall directly in front of Raul, where a video of Alex's torture session played on a loop. He could now hear the voice clearly but did not show any emotion.

"You have cost our city billions of dollars in the destruction of government property, and the penalty for this shall be death."

Years of intensive physical and guerrilla training in Freedom Now had prepared him for what lay ahead. Raul could do seventy-five to eighty push-ups in two minutes, one hundred sit-ups in two minutes, and fifteen pull-ups in four minutes without breaking a sweat. In addition to his physical prowess, Raul had an IQ of 170 and strong visual and mathematical abilities. He was considered one of the most dangerous members of his group.

"Where is your headquarters located?" Silence, followed by more questions.

"Give us the location and number of bases your organization holds. Whom do you report to?"

They alternated between hot and cold room temperatures, sleep and food deprivation, electrical shocks, and the video of Alex on loop.

Hours turned into days, but Raul gave nothing away. They decided to bring in Dr. Khan, a specialist in the most arcane forms of torture involving parts of the body that were the most sensitive to intense pain, such as the eardrums, teeth, and the underside of the eyelid. After several weeks, Dr. Khan reported back to the board:

"Gentlemen, this is incredible; most of my subjects died after enduring the pain I have inflicted on Santiago."

Mohamed, the board's president said,

"Is it really possible to die from pain? Anyway, whether it is or not, this is a waste of valuable time."

Dr. Regunath said,

"Not necessarily. Raul may be exactly the type of soldier we need."

Frustrated, the New City Department of Safety Enforcement decided it was time to move Raul to the Life Never Ends facility. They first sedated him and then bathed and dressed him in clean clothes.

. . .

On the day of the move, Raul Santiago looked like any ordinary New City resident. He recognized the IS-shaped buildings as they approached their destination. Raul had committed to memory the floor plans of every New City government building and was familiar with every square inch of the facility he was now entering. They entered the building through an arched silver door. The walls were painted white to create an illusion of calmness, comfort, and order, but the whiteness only enhanced the cold and sterile environment. The high ceilings were intended to make the building's rooms look large and spacious, but they only camouflaged the emptiness and hostile nature of the facility.

Raul was escorted to the holding area, where candidates were prepped for their procedure. Each candidate had his or her own private room equipped with furniture, a bathroom, and a telescreen. Raul was still sedated and would continue to be so until preparation for his transformation was completed.

The board of Life Never Ends held weekly meetings during which they decided the fates of the candidates admitted to the facility. The meeting started promptly at 9:00 a.m. that Monday. The board, like everything else in New City, was a facade; it was composed of representatives of the various groups that worked there: scientists, engineers, architects, and government leaders. After completing old business, President Mohamed said, "The next item on the agenda is to determine what the best procedure for Raul Santiago is."

The discussion about what to do with Raul had been going on for months now. New City needed his skill set; his training and abilities were invaluable for their armed forces as well as for their Law Enforcement Unit. This is the reason he had not been terminated.

Dr. Regunath insisted that Raul could be cloned. "My strongest inclination is to clone him; we have designed a near-perfect technique to remove, or shall I say, "knock out," the undesirable genetic traits that predispose Mr. Santiago toward impulsive and volatile behavior."

Mohamed was concerned that Raul's genetic makeup could not be altered. "Can you guarantee that this procedure will result in a risk-free product? We cannot afford any more loss of property."

Dr. Regunath said,

"Our clinical trials have shown a 99.9% success rate. We can insert DNA to target specific traits we wish to keep and enhance as well as target negative traits we want to remove."

A motion was made by Dr. Regunath and seconded by the lead engineer, Mr. Abdallah, to submit Raul Santiago to the transformation procedure. The motion was passed, and that afternoon, he was transferred to the subterranean level of the facility, which stored the stasis chambers. The engineers at the Life Never Ends facility had designed pods to sustain candidates undergoing various procedures the scientists had designed. Once the procedures were completed, the candidates were officially considered property of the government. Raul was placed in a stasis chamber for Model Double Helix XY, the first step of the cloning process. He would remain there for the next six months.

· · ·

The alarm was red and sounded like horns blaring. It alternated every five seconds with the announcement that a product had escaped from one of the pods. President Mohamed became enraged when his security detail informed him that it was Raul Santiago who had escaped from his stasis chamber. He started pacing back and forth and barking orders.

"I knew this would happen; that boy has cost us billions of dollars in property loss, and he is now loose in this facility. Find him now!"

But the head of security had not finished his report.

"Sir, there is something else."

"What?"

"It appears that several guards found him in the stairwell."

Mr. Mohamed's face was getting redder by the second. His eyes were protruding from their sockets, and the veins in his neck were bulging.

"Spit it out already, will you?! What happened?!"

"They tried to grab him, but he broke free and ran."

"Well what are you doing standing there?! Go get the security guards and bring them here to me now!"

The head of security was now trembling.

"Sir, I cannot get them now because they are all in the infirmary."

Raul had overpowered the three security guards who confronted him with his highly developed fighting skills, and he had outrun the rest of the security detail with his newly enhanced running speed.

Raul had been in the pod for several months when one of the technicians had forgotten to secure the latch after a routine check. However, the time spent in the stasis chamber was not achieving the desired results. That is, Raul's mind remained intact while his other physical attributes were being enhanced. He was becoming the super soldier New City wanted but could not controlled because Raul fell into that small percentage whose genetic makeup could not be altered.

While in the pod, Raul was conscious of everything, and when he was not sleeping, he spent the endless hours planning.

Raul was in the cave, training and listening to the instructions of his master—*"Remember that aggression can overcome many obstacles, but to tap into that aggression effectively, you must…"*—when he was awakened abruptly by the thump of the pod door closing. However, he did not hear the familiar clank of the latch.

Raul waited patiently until the footsteps had faded away and there was only silence. The technicians had completed their daily check of the pods.

He broke free, found the entrance to the stairwell, and ran up the flights of stairs until he had reached the top of the facility. Raul got as far the edge of the roof when he realized that the building was on a cliff; he saw the New City lights in the distance, but he had no way to get there.

What now? He decided to go back and had just started down the stairwell when he was accosted by three guards. After overpowering the security personnel, he took their weapons and continued down the flights of stairs until he reached the last level of the building. Raul searched his memory for the location of the vents he knew existed. He removed the grate and crawled into one of the narrow tunnels until he found the room that contained the generator that powered most of the facility. Raul used a knife he had taken from one of the guards to break the lock. Once inside, he could finally relax long enough to plan his next move.

Raul found himself in the bowels of the building, going over the basic principles of guerrilla warfare as his master's voice resonated in his mind, *"You use a strong, small surprise attack against a larger force. You turn your weaknesses into strengths: if you are hidden, then they are exposed. You fight only battles you can win. You take their weapons and use them against them."*

Raul needed to move quickly because he knew he did not have much time—twenty-four hours at best—because they would be looking for him. Although he was already near it, he knew it would not be enough to blow up the power generator; there was always the risk that the hard drive would be recovered. He must first stop at the maintenance department, located on the level above him, where he could get the necessary supplies to build explosive devices. Powerful improvised explosive devices could be made from products such as paint removers, drain cleaners, and rust removers. They contained nitric or sulfuric acid, either of which can be used to make high-order explosives.

Raul had already taken a uniform from one of the guards so that no one would suspect him. The maintenance technician waxing the floors in the corridor never saw Raul coming. He came up from behind and swiftly broke the technician's neck before severing his hand to get the biometric authentication he needed to gain access to the maintenance department. Once inside, he disabled the surveillance cameras. It took him very little time to assemble several explosive devices.

The main control room was located on the top floor of the building. Getting into the room where the CPU was located would be almost impossible because of the strict security measures used to protect it. Raul thought to himself that his timing would have to be precise; there would be no room for error. He waited a few moments before exiting, quickly checked the corridors to make sure no one was coming, and then made a wild dash for the stairwell because he could not run the risk of being detected. As he climbed the stairwell, he stopped on only certain floors to secure the explosives along the way.

. . .

Raul took a few minutes to get his breathing under control when he arrived at the entrance of the 103rd floor. At any given time, there were supposed to be three guards in the surveillance office monitoring the security of the main control room. Abraham was the only guard seated behind the monitoring screens at the precise moment that Raul was approaching the door to the control room. He had just turned his head away from the screen to retrieve his phone, which had slipped underneath the table.

Raul tightly grabbed one of the guards stationed outside the door and then turned him around to use as a shield. The second guard had his weapon in his hand within seconds of Raul's attack, but he ended up shooting the guard instead of Raul. In addition to the biometric authentication, several keys were needed to gain entrance. It took Raul several tries before he obtained the sequence to open the door. There were nine guards in the control room, but this did not matter because once Raul had located the CPU, he immediately detonated the explosives.

By the time Abraham had looked up at the screen, the two guards stationed outside the door were on the floor, dead. He initiated the security alarm just as Raul pushed the detonator in his hand.

CHAPTER SEVEN

Shardonay Jones Moves In

The train was delayed, Maria Elena looked at her watch as though she could will the train to get there faster. *I wish this damn train would hurry up and get here.* It was Christmas Eve in NYC and there were more passengers on the train than usual, many of the last minute shoppers trying to get home to their families. She was annoyed and thought to herself, *I cannot wait to get to the block and pick up some wings and fries at the chicken spot.*

Maria Elena was in her first year of law school and would arrive home at approximately eleven every night. She was sleep deprived and mentally exhausted from the long hours of reading. Most evenings Maria Elena would pass out as soon as she entered her apartment. She lived in the only apartment building in her neighborhood which was located between the chicken spot "Two Hot Wings" and "The Pitbull Lounge."

Maria Elena had an 18-hour a day schedule. She would get up at five in the morning, shower, and have a cup of coffee before the two hour commute to school, classes and the the endless hours of preparation for the next day of lectures. Four hours of sleep had become the norm, the line between being awake and asleep was becoming more blurry each day.

Because of the train delays, Maria Elena arrived at Two Hot Wings one hour later than usual.

"Hola Luzmar, how you doing?"

"Aqui mijita jodia y mal paga (Here, poorly paid and fucked.) but it ain't your fault. What are you doing here so late niña (girl) ?"

"My God those trains were brutal tonight. I thought I would never get home." Luzmar handed over the order of hot wings and fries.

"Feliz Navidad (Merry Christmas) Luzmar, see you Monday night."

"Felices fiestas, que la pases bien Maria (Have a good one, Happy Holidays, have a good one Maria).

. . .

Maria Elena first saw her going up the stairs. She was strikingly beautiful, curvacious body, luscious caramel skin with hazel eyes. Her red skirt swaying as she climbed the stairs to the third floor. To Maria Elena's surprise, the woman opened the door to the apartment next door. Her face broke out into the most beautiful smile Maria had ever seen.

Maria Elena was totally caught off guard when the woman spoke to her,

"What you got there, honey? Mmm...mmm, that sure do smell good."

At a loss for words,

"Ain't nothing but some wings."

The woman started laughing,

"Well, the person who made those wings must have sat on them.
. Hi, I'm Shardonnay, darling."

"Hello, I live next door, my name is Maria Elena."

"It's a pleasure to meet you darling."

And just like that Shardonnay disappeared into her apartment, leaving Maria Elena standing there. She thought to herself, *Que estupida* (how stupid). *Of course she had to know I live next door. Great... now my new neighbor thinks I'm an idiot.*

After dinner, Maria Elena called her mother to tell her that someone had finally moved into the apartment next door. There were only three apartments on each floor and that one had been vacant for over ten years since the tragic deaths of the Santiago family.

"Mama, a woman has moved next door."

Maria Elena's mother exclaimed,

"What! After all these years Pedro finally found a tenant. You know the spirits of those two women are still there."

"Hay mama por favor (please mother) those are superstitions, there are no such things as ghosts."

"Oh really, Ms. Attorney smarty pants? Todo el mundo (everyone) in this neighborhood knows the apartment is haunted. When you hear the new neighbor screaming don't say nothing."

"Oh for God"s sake Mama stop being so dramatic." Maria Elena exasperated with her mother decided to end their conversation,

"Buenas Noches Mama (Goodnight Mother, I will talk to you tomorrow)."

"Que dios the bendiga hija (God bless you daughter)."

. . .

Maria Elena returned to her apartment on Saturday at 10 in the morning. She had slept in after spending Christmas with family at her mother's house on Friday. Maria spent most of the day studying for her first final exams. Her stomach tied in knots from the anxiety. After hours of reviewing her study outlines and memorizing rules of law, she must have dozed off. Maria Elena woke up abruptly to the sound of jazz music. She heard the sound of muffled voices come through the wall. Maria Elena thought she heard the sound of man's voice but could not make out what they were saying. She heard the man's voice call something out and then heard clearly the distinctive sound of Shardonnay's laughter.

It appeared that Shardonnay was not around during the day because Maria Elena did not hear any voices nor sound of movement coming from her neighbor's home. It's a good thing that woman is never home during the day with all the reading I have to do. I have to pass these exams if I am to get that Fellowship at the end of my first year. However, Shardonnay was definitely home during the evenings and she was never alone.

. . .

Sunday was uneventful and Maria Elena followed her normal routine: up by 5 am, shower, coffee and studying with periodic breaks for meals. She had plenty of leftovers and looked forward to her pernil (roast pork) sandwiches, arroz con gandules (rice with pigeon peas) and her aunt's delicious potato salad.

Once again she heard nothing from her neighbor until she heard a soft knock at the door at about nine that evening. Maria Elena was startled because she never had any guests come over. Her social life was non existent since she had started law school. When she answered the door, Shardonnay was standing there wearing a beautiful shade of red that complimented her caramel colored skin with matching lipstick that complimented her beautiful smile.

"Honey, could you use some company? I been feeling kinda of lonely and thought you might like to chat."

Dumbfounded Maria Elena waved her in and said,

"Sure come in."

Shardonnay glided past Maria and quickly made herself at home as she sat down on the sofa.

Maria Elena said,

"Oh my where are my manners. May I offer you something to drink? I have some great Spanish White Wine that I got for Christmas."

Maria thought *Oh, what the hell it is the holidays after all!*

"Oh, I so do love to drink wine, darling."

Maria poured two glasses of wine and put them on the coffee table next to the bottle so she would not have to get up again. She made a toast,

"Feliz Navidad to my lovely new neighbor"

Shardonnay chuckled,

"Feliz Navidad to you darling."

"Where are you from Shardonnay?

"I'm from the Jones family in New Orleans. My family has lived there for generations."

"New Orleans? Girl that is a long way to come. Why the Bronx?"

Shardonnay just smiled,

"It was getting hard to find work back home, business is just not what it used to be."

"What do you mean? ".

"Why, darling, I'm a hard working girl."

Maria Elena was already feeling the effects of the wine as she had not had anything to drink in a long time because of her studies. She lost interest in Shardonnay's line of work and poured herself another glass of wine. Shardonnay seized the opportunity to asked Maria Elena about her studies and the conversation turned in another direction. Several hours and glasses of wine later, Maria Elena passed out on her sofa and never noticed Shardonnay's departure.

· · ·

To her horror Mafia Elena woke up at 12 noon on Monday with a splitting headache. The bottle of wine was left empty on the table and next to it was a full glass of wine. *Oh my God, I drank that bottle of wine by myself. At what time did the neighbor leave?* The previous night's event were a total fog. Maria decided to dismiss the incident because she had more important things to do. She got up took a shower, drank a cup of black coffee and resumed her daily routine. *Well, at least I don't have that long ass commute ahead of me this week.*

The music began like clock work around nine that evening but this time it was blues instead of jazz. Once again the muffled sound of voices and what sounded like singing. Maria Elena became annoyed and had a good mind to go knock on Shardonnay's door but decided against it because she did not dare. This continued for several nights in a row: the conversations, the music, clinking of glasses and laughter.

. . .

It was Thursday, New Year's Eve and Maria had decided to stay home because her final exams were the following week. Maria Elena could not take it any longer and knocked on Shardonnay's door to ask her to please keep the noise down. At first, she knocked softly but there was no answer. Maria became frustrated and began to knock harder on the door. The knocking woke up Doña Josefina who lived in the apartment across from her. Josefina opened her door and asked,

"Pero muchacha que tu haces a esta hora de la noche?(Girl what are you doing at this time of night)?

"Please forgive me Doña, I did not mean to disturb you." Maria Elena explained that she was going to ask Shardonnay to lower the music so she could study.

"Girl, have you lost your mind? No one has lived in that apartment for ten years!"

"What? Don't you hear the music?"

"Que musica…ni musica? (What music…there is no music)?" Maria Elena tried knocking one last time when all of sudden the door swung back. The apartment was empty. There was no Shardonnay, no music and no man. Doña Josefina looked at Maria with pity in her eyes,

"Mijita you better get some sleep, you are studying too hard/"

"Thank you Doña, good night."

Inside her apartment, Maria Elena collapsed on the floor. Maria get a grip now. You are not crazy. There must be an explanation for this. She remained in that position for several hours. But her rational mind could not come up with any explanation for what had just happened.

Maria Elena decided that it was best for her to forget to put the whole thing out of her mind for now. She finally fell asleep during the early morning hours thinking about Shardonnay.

. . .

Several weeks after her final exams, Maria Elena still could not get Shardonnay Jones out of her mind. She started to do some research and at her computer typed in: Shardonnay Jones, New Orleans, Louisiana. There it was, Shardonnay's beautiful smile and eyes looking back at her. It was an article about a young woman from a prominent family that had been found dead ten years ago. Although the family refused to comment, friends confirmed Shardonnay was disowned by her family because she had chosen a profession of ill repute. The circumstances surrounding her death remained a mystery.

CHAPTER EIGHT

The Day I Almost Died

On September 19, 1996, Dr. Francisco De La Esperenza checked out of the Atlanta Airport Marriott Gateway Hotel right after the Neuroradiology Conference. He was a renowned expert in his medical field and had just made a presentation on Vertebral Augmentation, a procedure to relieve pain where part of the spine had collapsed. The presentation was a success. The hotel clerk asked the doctor,

"Sir, how was your stay with us?"

" Everything went well, thank you."

It was his 36th birthday and he was anxious to get back to his family to celebrate. Francisco thought *it's a good thing I don't have to drive to the airport*. He arrived at his gate one hour before the scheduled departure time of 4 pm. The flight was delayed half hour because of foggy weather conditions. Once Francisco boarded the plane, the flight went smoothly and he arrived at Pittsburgh Airport without any further difficulties. He picked up his car, a Dodge Stealth, at the airport parking lot and prepared for the one and half hour trip.

Dr. Francisco De La Esperenza was on the Interstate 79 driving back home, listening to his favorite Bruce Springsteen song *Dancing In the Dark*. He was transported back to the days when he used to DJ for his friends at their house parties in "Little Puerto Rico."

It was dusk, Francisco was about 45 minutes away from his home in Morgantown. He was approaching the Washington, PA exit on I-79 when a tarp came flying out of nowhere and landed on his windshield. The driver behind Francisco looked on with horror at the car in front of him started moving to the right.

"Look at the car in front of us, it is going over the embankment!"

The car slowly swerved to the right, went over the embankment and rolled down the hill.

"Hurry! Call the highway police."

. . .

Several drivers had stopped at the side of the road. They saw Dr. Francisco De La Esperenza emerge from behind the embankment.

"Are you all right? We saw what happened!"

The state trooper arrived on the scene to a group of spectators surrounding a well dressed man. Dr. Francisco De La Esperenza was still wearing the white shirt, blue suit, and black shoes from the conference.

"Hello Sir, I'm Officer James. Where are the victims?"

Francisco replied,

"I am the victim. I am fine, there is nothing wrong with me."

They were interrupted by the sounds of the approaching sirens. The ambulance had been dispatched because they expected injured passengers. The state trooper looked confused,

"I'm sorry, what did you say? I was told a car went over the embankment."

Dr. Francisco De La Esperenza explained it was his car that went down the hill.

"Is this some kind of joke?'

Francisco did not have one scratch on him. Officer James thought, This man must be intoxicated. After administering the necessary sobriety tests and concluding that Dr. Francisco De La Esperenza was indeed sober, Officer James asked,

"Can you please tell me what happened here?'

. . .

"I could not see in front of me because the tarp covered my windshield completely. I hit my brakes but I felt the car moving to the right although it had slowed down. I thought to myself, Why is the car not stopping? At first I thought maybe the roads are slippery because of the fog. Then I realized, Oh, no the tarp has wrapped itself around the tires of the car. I felt the car going down a hill and all sudden it came to a complete stop. Did I hit something? Everything seemed to be happening in slow motion. I was stunned by the impact but did not lose consciousness. I was confused, the car was still moving, Bruce Springsteen was still playing. I realized the car is upside down because I undo my seat belt and I fall down. Oh my God, the car has flipped over. I turned the car off because I was afraid it would catch fire. I tried to get out but the door was jammed. I kept trying the door until it loosened and I was able to open it, and then climbed out."

. . .

That was the statement I gave Officer James, standing on the side of the road before the Washington, PA exit on I-79. It was the truth but not the entire truth. At the point of impact (I later found out my car hit a tree), I saw this tunnel of bright light, almost like fluorescent light. At the end of the tunnel, I saw a tall dark hooded figure, he moved his hand from left to right as if signaling "No." There was a strange smell in the car, it smelled like death. This is what prompted me to turn the car off. I was afraid the car would catch fire. I tried to get out but the door was jammed. I started praying, *God, please don't let it end like this, not like this*. The door that had been jammed, now opened and then I crawled out. I came out of the car without a scratch.

. . .

The Flatbed truck came to pick up the Dodge Stealth which had been completely crushed during the accident, it was now flattened. When I returned home, my wife did not believe that I was in an accident until the following day when I picked up my personal belongings and she saw the car.

CHAPTER NINE

The Night I Met BB Hatchet

It was 96 degrees that summer night in NYC and the temperature in in the Beam Theater was not much cooler in spite of the air conditioning. On that evening, there were over 2000 students seated in the auditorium studying for the Bar Examination. This was a grueling experience equivalent in pain only to torture. John Lance would state the rule of law and the students would write it in their notebooks. This same rote exercise was repeated hour after hour as though they were in trance, and writing the rule in the notebook became a robotic exercise.

Maria Elena was sitting next to her best friend Giovanni -often referred to as her "law school husband." She was lost in the reverie that was her latest lover Camilo Sixto. In the distance, Maria Elena heard the drone of John Lance's voice repeating the rule of law for the equitable distribution of marital property in a divorce proceeding,

"Each spouse is entitled to half of any property or assets acquired during the marriage."

This statement woke everyone up and the students sat up straight in their seats for the first time since the beginning of the lecture. One of the students asked,

"Are the earnings of a law practice started during marriage subject to equitable distribution?"

The answer was an unequivocal,

"Yes."

Maria Elena thought, It is best not to start a law practice after one gets married. I'm never going to get marry, so it really doesn't matter. In fact, one day Maria Elena would marry. However, she would never start a law practice.

The nightly four hour lecture went by rather quickly although it was an arduous and tedious task. Soon Giovanni and Maria Elena were getting their backpacks ready for the trek back to the Bronx. Every evening after class, they would walk to the subway and take the train together. The train ride took. almost two hours because they first had to go downtown to Grand Central Station to switch over to east side number 6 train going to the Bronx. Maria Elena was impatient,

"I hate taking this train at night it takes forever."

"Oh, stop complaining already…will you?"

Her response was drowned out by the train as it pulled into the station. Once seated, Giovanni would pull out his index cards and start studying. Maria Elena thought, *There he goes again, all he does is study. Mamao* (sucker).

Giovanni only accompanied Maria Elena through half of her journey. Once the train arrived in the Bronx, he would walk a few blocks to his apartment in the Park Square Houses. But Maria Elena would have to take a bus to get home, this often meant another hour of travel and one hour less of much needed sleep. So instead, she would take a $3.00 cab ride which would leave her at her front door in 10 minutes. The cabs would line up outside the entrance of the train station.

Upon exiting the train station, she said her farewell to Giovanni and as customary walked towards the first cab on line. It was at this time that she first heard the voice,

"Maria Elena do not get into that car."

Instinctively she pulled away from the first car and started walking towards the second cab on line. However, the driver from the first car intercepted Maria Elena. It was hard to avoid this man that stood about six feet tall, as he smiled and politely asked,

"Do you need a cab madam?"

Maria Elena looked up at the man and felt sorry for him. She rationalized It's really not fair since he was the first on line, it was rightfully his turn.

"Okay."

And so she got into BB Hatchet's cab and he closed the door behind her. This was the first mistake that almost cost Maria Elena her life.

The ride from the subway station to Maria Elena's house was approximately one half of a mile. Within a few minutes the car pulled in front of her house. She gave the cab driver the usual $3.00 fare but the driver said that the fare was $4.00. The argument began over the amount of the fare. The driver insisted,

"This is $4.00 fare."

Maria Elena protested,

"No, but I always pay $3.00."

It was here that things took a turn for the worst. The driver yelled,

"You are trying to screw me and I won't even let my own mother screw me!"

This was the second mistake that almost cost Maria Elena her life. BB then quickly made a U turn and headed back up White River Road to the train station. He was livid with anger as he continued to rant ,

" I rather take you back to the train station than to let you screw me out my money!"

BB had no intention of returning the train station, indeed he was a very angry man.

Bob Brown (BB) was born in a small southern town to a young unmarried mother who was unable to love and nurture him because she was too busy trying to escape the stigma of having a child out of wedlock. He was Loretta Brown's first born son and they both lived with his grand parents. Loretta met another man, he was a deputy who worked for the local Sheriff's office. At the age of 5, BB's mother Loretta got married and subsequently had five more children, all boys. Instead of things getting better with his mother's new found happiness, the situation worsen for BB. Whereas before he was simply ignored, now he was both ignored and blamed for everything that went wrong including all of his brothers misdeeds. In short, his new father ran his household like a boot camp and his submissive mother continued to be emotionally absent from his life.

Instead of continuing on White River Road toward the train station, BB decided to make an immediate right unto the White River Road Expressway. Maria Elena's heart was pumping rapidly and thoughts began to wildly run through her mind as she quickly began to realize that the man behind the wheel was insane. In a moment of clarity , she realized that he was not returning to the train station. Oh my God this man is crazy and he is not going back to the station. Dios mio ayudame (God please help me). And just as this thought crossed her mind, BB turned unto the ramp that was the entrance to the expressway. At this point, Maria Elena was in full panic mode, she knew she had only seconds to do something or she was going to die. This was the second time she heard the voice,

" Jump."

This time, Maria Elena did not hesitate, she opened right hand side door and jumped out.

. . .

At about two a.m, Maria Elena woke up briefly on the gurney at the Jacob's Hospital Emergency Room. Everything was a blur and she could barely make out the faces of her mother and brother looming over her. She was awake long enough to notice the tears streaming down her brother's face and the look of helplessness in his eyes.

Several hours later, the doctors at Jacob's Memorial Hospital were making their morning rounds. Maria Elena was under the heavy sedation of Demerol and the doctor's voices seemed far away,

"Here we have a 27 year old female who was found last night by the police walking on the shoulder of the highway. Although she was walking, she was unconscious and oblivious to her surroundings. When questioned by the officer, she was not able to tell them her name or how she got there."

In addition to the head concussion, Maria Elena had suffered second degree burns to about one third of her body including the right side of her face, her arms and legs. The friction burns were caused by the asphalt covering the shoulder of the highway.

Camilo Sixto was standing outside of Maria Elena's Hospital Room, his worst fears had come true, that Maria Elena would get hurt in the streets because she was too trusting. Remembering the countless arguments he had about carrying a weapon for her self-defense. Going over in his mind the endless conversations. Camilo had purchased a dagger for Maria Elena to carry when she left the law school late at night for self-defense

"This is for you to carry in your boot."

She refused,

"I hate weapons and have no intention of carrying a knife." Camilo persisted,

"Maria you need this, those streets in Newark are very dangerous at night."

"No, I don't think is necessary for me to carry a knife."

Camilo asked,

"Why not?"

"For god sake,I'm attending law school. How would it look, me carrying a dagger in my boot?"

He continued,

"It's for your protection. Come on babe, please is for your safety."

"Please Camilo stop, your making me crazy!"

...

Maria Elena finally woke up that night about 3 a.m. to find a nurse standing by her bedside. It was not a face of compassion that stared back at her but one of morbid curiosity. The nurse said,

"What were you thinking when you jumped out that car? Don't you know you could have killed yourself?"

It was the accusation that confused Maria Elena since she believed in her heart that she had jumped to saved her life. She did not respond.

It was a slow and painful recovery that entailed heavy dosages of Demerol and intensive Hydrotherapy. Camilo was there day after day to watch the excruciating treatments and take care of Maria Elena as he always did. Several weeks later Maria Elena was released from the Burn Unit of Jacob's Memorial Hospital. The police did nothing to apprehend the man that had done this to her, they never even conducted an interview to ascertain the facts.

...

One year, two months, and three days later; Camilo Sixto got into the back seat of the first cab waiting on line outside the Park Square train station. The days were getting cooler so Camilo rolled down his window and gave the driver directions to his destination. One block away from the passenger's destination, the driver stopped for a red light. Slowly Camilo raised his right hand placed a Glock 17 to the back of BB Hatchet's head, as he leaned forward he quietly whispered another set of instructions into his ear.

"Take the White River Road Expressway 95 North to Exit 8B, Hart Island, make a right after the drawbridge (there is a sign) and take the second turn at the traffic circle."

Before approaching the drawbridge, Camilo quickly said to the driver,

"Make a right here."

There was a small detour leading to a dark and abandoned area. Upon arrival BB Hatchet was instructed to get out of his car. There was another vehicle waiting for them in the shadows. Camilo and his friends drove that night for about three hours. When they arrived at their agreed upon location, they dragged BB Hatchet out of the back seat of the car. One of the men handed BB a can of gasoline,

"I want you to pour this over yourself."

Camilo saw the look of horror,

"What? Did you think I was going to shoot you?"

BB finally found his voice when he realized what they planned for him.

"Why are you doing this?"

Camilo responded,

"You heard the man, pour it over yourself."

BB could not move, he felt the warm liquid going down the inside of his pants. Camilo took a shot but intentionally missed. The driver picked up the can and shakily poured the gas over himself. Once again BB asked,

"Why are you doing this? I don't know you." As soon as the can dropped on the floor, Camilo said,

"You tried to screw me and I won't even let my own mother screw me!"

When Camilo saw the look of recognition, he threw his lit cigarette in the direction of the driver.

CHAPTER TEN

The Patient In Bed 508(1)

Mercenaria Santiago's family was at a loss for words when the registration clerk at the Lower Bellville Sanitarium said,

"Sorry Mrs.Santiago we are filled to capacity, I'm afraid we are going to have to refer her to the NYC Downtown Memorial Hospital."

Earlier that evening, Mercenaria Santiago had once again attempted to jump out of her bedroom window. It had taken three family members to subdued her, while the youngest member of the family dialed 911.

Unbeknownst to the staff at the NYC Downtown Memorial Hospital, the patient in Bed 508(1) had been in and out of mental institutions since childhood. She had been misdiagnosed by the school Psychologist as having a major depressive disorder which is often characterized by an all-encompassing low mood and is usually accompanied by low self-esteem. The first incident occurred when she was just six years old. She laid flat on the floor of her class room at dismissal time, refusing to move and thus wreaking havoc with the smooth administration of the school.

...

They brought the new patient in on Tuesday about three in the morning. The nurse pulled the curtain separating their beds. Hope greeted Sophia,

"Good Morning Mrs.Santos." She then closed the curtains separating the beds. Hope began the usual artillery of questions.

"How tall are you?" A female voice responded,

"Five feet, six inches"

"How much do you weigh?" There was a long period of silence followed by a slow screeching noise as the scale was dragged across the floor over to the bed. Sophia heard Hope say,

"Okay, 306 lbs."

She thought that this might be a good time to take the slow painful walk around the curtain to find out the identity her new room mate. It was a strange, round, yet, familiar face that stared back at Sophia from Bed 508 (1), her head covered by a mop of black curly hair, the small black piercing eyes, and facial hair. Where had she seen it before? But of course in that Science Fiction movie. The patient in Bed 508 (1) looked just like one those creatures. Wait! No, there was something terribly wrong. There was a cloud of darkness surrounding that face and a coldness emanating from that body that she would never forget. Sophia could not describe the uneasiness she was experiencing except to say that she was clearly and without a doubt in the presence of evil.

Hope then sat on a chair at the entrance of the hospital room once she completed her routine examination of the patient. Sophia continued her slow but excruciating walk, while holding unto the IV pole, towards the nurses' station. She immediately informed the head nurse in charge that she believed the patient in Bed 508 (1) was extremely dangerous. Sophia explained,

"I am a sensitive and see these things. I know that what I am telling you is hard to believe. But this woman is going to hurt someone here tonight."

The head nurse said,

"My dear Mrs.Santos just because a person is a danger to themselves does not necessarily mean that she is a danger to others as well."

"Please listen to me. If a patient is a danger to herself, there is a high probability that she can in fact be a danger to others as well."

Despite Sophia's repeated protestations, he would not concede that this patient was in fact dangerous. The question was left unanswered as to why there was someone guarding the patient in Bed 508 (1) if she was not a threat to others? Sophia does not remember how long she stayed at the nurses' station but eventually she was coaxed into returning to her room where she remained wide awake until the very early morning. She could not shake the fear that had now taken residence in the very core of her soul. The fact that Hope was stationed at the front door of the room did little to console her.

. . .

It was 6:00 am, Sophia heard the usual movements of the hospital staff and decided it was time to go for a another walk, only to discover that Hope was sound asleep at her post. Yet the patient in Bed 508 (1) was staring darkly into space. She felt a cold chill run from the top of her head to the bottom of her feet. Sophia murmured to herself,

"This is not good, not good at all."

She felt compelled to wake up the nurses' aide whose head laid on top of the books she had been studying.

"Hope, are you watching the television or is the television watching you?" Sophia glanced in the direction of the patient in Bed 508 (1). Hope reassured her that there was nothing to worry about because the patient in Bed 508 (1) had been "sedated." She too seemed totally unaffected by the presence of that woman.

When Sophia returned, she found someone had relieved Hope from her post. The television was on and the patient in Bed 508 (1) appeared to be peacefully watching the show. She could not help but wonder what was transpiring in the mind behind those demonic eyes. During the course of the day, the nurses would come and go. Claire the day nurse came in to conduct an examination. She closed the curtains separating the beds once again. Claire asked,

"Do you hear voices of persons that are not in the room?" The patient in Bed 508 (1) simply responded.

"No."

It was all Sophia could do not to burst out laughing. "How absolutely absurd, as though she would actually say *'Yes, madam, I hear the voices of persons not present in the room.'*"

The day progressed and was rather uneventful. However, Sophia watched her room mate closely because she feared for safety. She noticed the patient in Bed 508 (1) would periodically get up to use the bathroom and then come right back to her bed. Sophia found this odd only because the patient in Bed 508 (1) had not eaten or drank anything since her admission at 3:00 am. The bathroom was located immediately adjacent to the front door of the room where the nurses' aide was stationed. Sophia continued to feel the heaviness in that room.

. . .

At 3:00 pm, twelve hours after Mercenaria's admission, Lia Lo arrived to relieve the nurses' aide seated outside the front door of room 508. Sophia experienced a feeling of dread in the pit of her stomach. Lia was a small frame Asian woman about 4' 10" tall who weighed no more than 100 pounds. She was a good, a warm and kind hearted woman who helped many of the patients, visiting them often with daily words of encouragement and prayers. All of sudden, an inexplicable fear overcame Sophia when she realized that Lia was expected to keep watch over the monster that was the patient in Bed 508 (1). Once again, she went to the front desk and voiced her concerns,

"I believed the patient in Bed 508 (1) to be extremely dangerous."

Only to have the clerk quickly dismiss her by reiterating the very words of the head nurse earlier,

"Do not worry. Just because a person is a danger to themselves does not mean that she is a danger to others." Sophia walked away asking herself,

"How could I get the staff to understand that they were putting themselves, other hospital employees, and the patients at risk."

Upon returning to her room, Sophia sat with Lia for several hours making small talk because she did not know what else to do. While she contemplated what to do next, it quickly became apparent to Sophia that Lia was extremely nervous when she started to catalog all the crazy patients that had been assigned to her. Mrs. Low went on to describe the day that Mr. Prickly had to be restrained because he had wandering hands and often would try to fondle the nurses' aides when they were bathing him or feeding him.

"They always give me the crazy patients. I had to untie that nasty man's hands and he slapped me, like that right on my face!"

Mrs. Lo could not sit still, was uneasy, and her anxiety grew with the passage of time.

· · ·

Around 6:00 pm, Sophia left Lia's side to go have dinner. Shortly thereafter the commotion began, she over heard foot steps running in the hallways, and voices yelling. Amongst what sounded like mass confusion, Sophia heard someone shout,

"Hey you! Where are you going?!" Then another person screamed,

"No she went that way!"

One of the nurses pointed to stairwell. The security guards arrived too late. They did not know that the patient in Bed 508 (1) had disappeared into the stairwell that was diagonally across from their room. The stairwell that could be seen quite clearly from the bathroom. The security guards ran down the stairs thinking that the patient was trying to escape!

· · ·

The call came in about 6:45 pm,

"Any units in the Chinatown area?"

Officer Wong responded to the call,

"Unit 551. we are one block south of Williams Street." The First Police Precinct dispatcher instructed them,

"Proceed to the New York Memorial Hospital Fifth Floor, we have a jumper." Johnson who was sitting next to Wong said,

"Oh shit, here we go. I hate these fucking cases." The officers arrived to the fifth floor of the hospital shortly after.

"Good evening madam I'm Officer Wong and this is Officer Johnson, are you the one who made the call to 911? We are here to investigate this matter." The head nurse, Destania who was was in a state of shock screamed,

"Investigate?! There is nothing to investigate, they are dead, both of them are dead."

"Can you tell us what happened?" It was all too much for Destania who broke down and started crying,

"You have to speak with Miguel, he saw the whole thing."

"And where may we find Miguel now?'

Destania pointed to the employee break room. The officers found Miguel sitting alone at a table, He was staring down at the coffee cup in front him, As they approached him they noticed that he was trembling. Officer Johnson spoke softly,

"May we talk to you for a few moments Sir"

Miguel nodded and pointed to the empty chairs next to him.He was the nurses' aide who went after Mercenaria when she ran into the stairwell. He was a large man and without his uniform had been mistaken for a wrestler on more than one occasion. The officers sat down and began their questioning.

"It is our understanding that you saw Ms, Santiago go into the stairwell?'

"I heard the alarm, I asked Destania What is going on? Destania was upset said a patient had ran out of her room, that she was trying to escape, But I didn't get there on time.

"What do you mean you didn't get there on time?"

"The guards got there after me, they decided to go down because they thought she was trying to escape, So I decided to up. When I got to the top , I saw the door to the roof was opened." Miguel stopped and took a drink. He kept shaking his head and muttering to himself,

"There was no way man…no way man." The officers waited for the Miguel to calm down. Officer cautiously asked,

"What happened next?"

"I heard the scuffle, that is when I saw them…"

"You saw them?"

"I saw Lia was holding the ankles, trying to stop the lady from going over the edge of the roof. Man that would have been impossible. Poor little Lia trying to stop that big lady, No way man." The two Officers looked at each other in disbelief.

"I ran across the roof as fast I could but I didn't get there on time."

Miguel watched the dark eyes of the patient in Bed 508 (1) as she together with Lia Lo descended six flights down.

. . .

Dr. Flores was conducting his morning rounds. He was about to walk into Room 508 to check on his patients when he stopped to talk to one of the nurses.

Sophia was in a total state of shock because nothing could have prepared her for what happened to Mercenaria Santiago. She overheard Dr. Flores telling one of the nurses that the patient in bed 508 (1) suffered from a severe form of schizophrenia in that she often heard voices telling her to jump and take her family with her in order to avoid eternal damnation.

In fact, Mercenaria had told the admitting doctor at the NYC Downtown Memorial Hospital that she had heard those very same voices earlier that evening when she attempted to jump from the balcony of her apartment located on the seventh floor.

CHAPTER ELEVEN

There Are Ghosts Living In My House

Rosa was not sure when she first heard the noises coming from the walls. Sometimes she heard what she thought was scratching from the floors—often in the middle of the night. There was a squirrel living in a tree in the backyard. Rosa would often see it scurrying around on her roof. At first she thought, *Could it be that the squirrels have moved into the attic?*

Rosa lived in an old house down the street from "El Callejón" (the alley), together with her husband of fifty years, Ramon. The house had been in her family since 1935. Over the years it had become financially difficult to maintain the large house, so the second floor had been closed. Rosa told Ramon about the noises, but Ramon slept like a log and insisted that he did not hear anything.

"It is all in your head..."

Over breakfast one morning, Rosa convinced her husband to go into the attic and check for intruders. Despite his protests, Ramon ultimately decided to do it to get his wife off his back.

"All right, all right, I will do it. But only if you stop nagging me. I don't want to hear one more word about this craziness." Ramon climbed the stairs to the attic and looked around. When he came down, he told Rosa,

"Okay. I checked and found nothing. Now stop bothering me."

• • •

Over the next few weeks, Rosa continued to hear the noises. It was maddening; she knew she was not crazy. Then one day she thought, *Maybe we have mice in the house.*

Rosa decided to call the exterminator. The exterminator arrived and asked,

"What is the problem?" Rosa explained that she had been hearing scratching noises coming from the wall.

"Well, let me take a look around the house first."

As the exterminator headed up the stairs, Rosa told him there was no one living on the second floor. After scanning the second floor, he then checked the attic. Fifteen minutes later, the exterminator reappeared downstairs.

"I need to inspect your bedroom and the bathroom."

Upon a thorough inspection of the house, the exterminator did not find any mice or any other type of vermin.

• • •

One night, Rosa was awakened by a loud thump. She was so startled that she almost fell out of her bed. As her heart beat wildly, she thought, *Oh my God! There are ghosts in this house.*

In addition to the noises, Rosa noticed strange signs around the house. For instance, there was the morning she found the teapot on the kitchen counter. She always kept the teapot on the stove. Ramon had simply dismissed her when she asked if he had made tea.

"Are you crazy? You know I don't drink tea."

Another time, she found a pair of Ramon's socks at the bottom of the stairs. Rosa knew no one would believe her. There was no one to talk to about this. *What do I do now?*

Rosa remembered that her cousin Sophia once mentioned going to a "Botanica" Religious Articles Store after she had been discharged from the hospital. She had insisted that the spirit of a dead "chinita" (Chinese woman) had followed her home. Rosa decided it was time to do some research. In the afternoon, she called a cab and took a quick ride to *Mama Chola*, the local Botanica.

She purchased a manual titled "*How to Get Rid of Negative Spirits and Other Entities,*" and all the necessary supplies to conduct a complete spiritual cleansing of her home.

· · ·

Rosa arrived back at her house ready to start the cleansing ritual when she heard what sounded like someone snoring.

Could it be that Ramon had fallen asleep? But Ramon had left around noon to go play dominoes with his friends at the bodega on the corner.

And the snoring was coming from the second floor. Rosa got the keys and painfully climbed the stairs. She quietly opened the front door and looked around but saw nothing. She followed the sound of snoring to a locked door. She had forgotten about the room her father kept locked so the children would not go in and play with his expensive equipment.

Rosa opened the door and, to her dismay, found a man in a sleeping bag on the floor. There was a microwave oven on a table in the corner and a small refrigerator next to it. And, unbelievably, there was a flat screen television against the wall. The man had made himself quite comfortable in Rosa's home.

CHAPTER TWELVE

Whatever Happened to El Brujo?

Princesa was sitting in Luzmar's kitchen applying an ice pack to her left eye while describing the previous evening's events. Princesa and Luzmar had been neighbors in the *Callejón* (the alley) located in the Little Puerto Rico section of the community for many years now. Luzmar had nursed Princesa during the aftermath of fights she had with Carlos.

Princesa was crying, "Carlos came home drunk again last night and slapped me and flung me across the room." In between sobs she described how Carlos, enraged with jealousy, started accusing her of having an affair with Jaime. He kept insisting that their baby was not his and threatened to kill Jaime where ever he found him.

Carlos inherited his father's bad temper that was only exacerbated by his persistent drinking and continuous cocaine use. Luzmar while consoling Princesa thought about the night she caught her man Rodolfo with that ho Zoraida. Luzmar was familiar with the type of jealous rage that would only lead to tragedy. Carlos was the oldest of Arturo's five sons; he was named after his father's youngest brother who died in an ill-fated accident at a very young age. It was said that Arturo never forgave himself for his brother's death. Arturo fled his town of Buena Vista in the early 1970's and settled in "little Puerto Rico", shortly thereafter he met and married Esperenza after a brief courtship.

Arturo worked as a doorman for a building in mid-town Manhattan and after several years was able to purchase one of the bungalows in "little Puerto Rico" for $6,000. These houses were once only summer bungalows but because of its geographic location, it became the home of the Puerto Ricans who moved into the community. The narrow streets, alley ways, and small houses surrounded by iron wrought fences were nostalgic of their long lost home. The bungalows could be bought for "china verdes" (dirt cheap). It took Arturo almost ten years of hard work and sweat to rebuild the bungalow into a habitable home. Carlos together with his four brothers were born and raised in this house.

Princesa was the only child born to Pedro and Lourdes late in life. When Princesa was born, Lourdes believed that she had been blessed by the Virgin Mary since she had not been able to bear any children in the fifteen years of marriage to Pedro. Lourdes was so grateful to the Virgin Mary for giving her Princesa that she never missed mass on Sundays, where she would recite the holy novena to Our Lady of Mercy in gratitude for the miracle she had been granted. However, fate played a bad hand on Pedro and Lourdes and one night while driving home from church, a drunken driver hit the car and both died upon impact.

Princesa was the only named beneficiary on the $500,000 Insurance Policy and the deed of the house, the only real estate owned by her parents, Pedro and Lourdes Ramos. A few days after the funeral, Carlos and Princesa moved into the house and made it their own. At the beginning it was like a fairy tale, they had their very own home where they could raise their two daughters (Esperanza and Esmeralda). They were so happy to have finally come into their own, that life became a perpetual celebration in which alcohol and cocaine played a prominent role. The late night parties would often last until the early morning hours and within a couple a years the money was almost all but gone.

Carlos' continued drug use resulted in his absenteeism from his employment. Eventually he lost his job which in turn made him more dependent on alcohol and cocaine. The drug abuse made him angry, paranoid and violent. Thus, the sporadic arguments and fights became a daily occurrence in the Santiago household and Princesa the target of Carlos' jealous tirades. He would often accuse her of sleeping with other men.

"I know your are sleeping with that fucking faggot." Carlos would yell and everyone would whisper that he was at it again. The fights were common knowledge and most neighbors feared for Princesa's safety.

Luzmar would often advise Princesa to leave Carlos, "Nena, he is going to kill you one day if you don't leave him." In order to prove her point, Luzmar told Princesa of the incident that had taken place a few months earlier with a member of Carlos' family. "The whole family is crazy. Don't you remember what 'la prima loca' (that crazy cousin) Mercenaria of his did?"

Princesa who was more often than not confused from the beatings said, "No."

"Bendito sea Dios (for the love of God), mija esa loca threw herself off the hospital roof but not before taking that poor little chinita (Chinese woman) with her!"

· · ·

Princesa, like most of the lonely women in the neighborhood, spent a lot of time on the internet in order to forget the daily physical abuse she endured.. She met Jaime, El Brujo, on a website called "Todos Juntos- A Great Place for Good People To Meet." El Brujo had a page solely dedicated to his spiritual practice where he would give readings, advice and prescribed rituals to mostly lonely and defeated housewives like Princesa. She had been a member of Todos Juntos for several months when she decided to visit El Brujo's page in order to get a reading. Princesa was desperate and was hoping that he could tell how to get out of her horrible situation. It was customary for the person requesting the reading to send a photo to El Brujo. He explained that he needed this in order to get in touch with that person's aura and determine the true source of the problem.

The day El Brujo received Princesa's photo he fell in love. "Oh my God, were his eyes deceiving him? Jaime fell into a trance," She was the most beautiful woman he had ever seen."

It was at this moment in time that Jaime decided that he would make Princesa his using every method available to him. On the spiritual plane, El Brujo proceeded to utilize every ritual he knew to secure Pricensa's love, sparing no expense. He prepared a special offering of Yellow sunflowers, honey and perfume to Oshun (the Goddess of Love). Jaime then offered Anaisa (the Spirit of Love) yellow roses, her favorite perfume, and jewelry. Finally El Brujo and prepared a strong ritual of love by dressing red love candles to be accompanied by the daily Tobacco Prayer in order to always keep you in your beloved's mind.

On the physical plane, Jaime showered Princesa with nothing but love and attention.He spoke to her daily professing his love and reassuring her that he would always be there to take care of her. "Good Morning my love, how are you feeling today?"

Princesa could not believe her good fortune, " Thank you so much for the beautiful flowers you sent."

· · ·

After several weeks of video chatting, texting and e-mailing back and forth, Jaime and Princesa decided to meet. On the day they were to meet. Princesa could barely contain her excitement.

"Luzmar, I cannot wait to meet Jaime, he is so fine."

Luzmar once again warned Princesa to be careful, "If Carlos finds out he is going to kill you both."

There were only a few persons in the coffee shop that afternoon. Jaime was patiently waiting for her when Princesa spotted him sitting at the back of the shop. Jaime convinced Princesa, who was so defeated by her circumstances that she would believe anything he had to say, that they were soul mates and it was for this reason that she could never be happy with Carlos.

"You know that I have loved you many lifetimes and we are meant to be together throughout eternity. If you stay with Carlos he will continue to beat you. He is never going to change babe. Please give me a chance to make you happy. "

It was at this meeting that Jaime proposed a plan to Princesa. He suggested that she leave Carlos and they go away together.

Princesa was terrified of her husband, " He is crazy and will not rest until he finds me, There will be no place to hide."

She explained that Carlos lived in Buena Vista for almost six years selling drugs and was ruthless in his business dealings, "You don't know what he is like, He once told me that a customer owed him a lot of money. Carlos tied the man up to a chair and chopped of his fingers with a machete."

Also, though never formally charged, she had heard many rumors in the barrio that he had killed several men who owed him money. But Jaime reassured Princesa that he had already started looking for a place where no one would be able to find them, not even Carlos.

. . .

There was a small but growing Puerto Rican community in the mountains of Knoxville Tennessee. They would gather at the Romano Pizza Shop located in the Cedars Bluff Mall on Wednesdays known as San Juan Night. The owner had moved there from the Bronx forty years earlier when his wife had secured a teaching position at the University of Tennessee. The Pizzeria had been in Enzo's family since 1915. So when he relocated to Knoxville he moved the business there with him. It was here that Jaime's cousin Jesus would attend the weekly meetings held by "I Will Survive", a preparedness group. Here the group would plan their activities to achieve their ultimate goal that is to be prepared in the event of a disaster. I Will Survive had purchased certain plots of land located in the mountains and where in the process of building shelters. Jesus was the owner of one of these plots. Jesus had received several calls from Jaime who had expressed a very strong interest in joining the group. Jaime explained that life in NYC had become too stressful for him and his soon to be wife. They both longed for the relaxing lifestyle of the South where they could spend long leisurely hours sitting on the porch sipping lemonade. Jesus had not heard from Jaime since he had left the Bronx ten years ago. It was hard for him to believe that Jaime wanted to move down south.

Jaime insisted, " Come on bro, I will pay you whatever you want, name your price."

Although suspicious of his cousin's motives, Jesus accepted Jaime's offer because he needed the money to finish building and equipping the bunker. At that week's I Will Survive meeting, Jesus presented his cousin's proposal. Although the group was leery about accepting a stranger, they trusted Jesus' judgment and accepted Jaime as a new member into their organization. Just as promised, Jaime had found the place where no one would be able to find them. He wasted no time in calling Princesa to give her the good news.

. . .

It was decided that the best time for Princesa to leave was while Carlos was out drinking. They hurriedly packed their belongings in two duffle bags that Luzmar had given her earlier that afternoon.

Luzmar who feared for Princesa's safety quickly shoved clothes into bags in order to get them out as quickly as possible, "Hurry, please!"

Jaime had called for the cab 10 minutes before the scheduled time of departure. They arranged for Jaime to take the cab and then pick up Princesa and the children in front of the house.

The girls kept asking "Where are we going mama?"

When they heard the sound of the horn honking, everyone froze. Princesa and the children quickly slipped out of the house, piled into the back of the cab with only a few meager belongings. Princesa left her house, heart racing, with her two daughters Esperanza and Esmeralda at 1:00 am. The cab traveled only a short distance to where they would pick up the van that would take the newly formed family to their final destination.

The van was now on 1-78 West, the children had fallen asleep in the back and Princesa was shaking in her seat next Jaime.

"You have to take it easy babe, we are going to be far away by the time he realizes you are gone."

But she was having visions of Carlos and the things he would do if he caught them. "This is a bad idea, a very bad idea. What time is it? It is not too late to turn back. Please lets go back."

Jaime continued to reassured Princesa as he took the Harrisburg exit to I-81 South, "No, we are not going back. I promise you we will be safe. We have a long trip ahead of us, please try to get some sleep."

During the 11 hour trip, they only made three stops to eat and use the bathroom. Jaime pulled up in front of the house located at 601 Summit Hill, just in time for lunch.

. . .

Carlos arrived and immediately sensed there was something wrong because there were no lights on in the house. He walked into the home searching for his wife but the living room and bedroom were empty. The laptop sat on the kitchen table in silence. Then he looked into his daughters' bedroom but the twin beds were both still made. When Carlos realized that his family was gone, a fear from the very core caused him to yell in terror. It was exactly 5:55 am when the neighbors in the callejon heard the scream that sounded much like that of a wounded animal. Carlos started screaming and sobbing. His mind raced wildly from one thought to another,

"Oh my god someone has taken my family!"

His worst fear had come true. The threats he had received so frequently before he fled Buena Vista came rushing back,

"We are going to kill everyone in your family you son of bitch!"

Carlos was pacing the floor frantically back and forth,

"Mother fucker, we will hunt you down and kill you like the animal you are."

Crying aloud in his drunken stupor,

"They are going to kill my wife and daughters."

Carlos had fled from Buena Vista after the DEA started closing in on his drug operation for the sale and distribution of cocaine. He had taken too many risks and made too many enemies, for instance, he did not know that he had mutilated the nephew of one of Buena Vista's Police Commanders.

It was the Commander that instructed his nephew to become an informant for the DEA, "I'm going to make sure that "hjio de la gran puta" (motherfucker) pays for what he did to you."

When Carlos learned of his impending arrest, he took the first plane out Luis Muñoz Marín International Airport to La Guardia.

Carlos finally passed out from exhaustion on the living room sofa. The room was dark, the heat stifling with only a ceiling fan, the air in the room oppressive. He tied José to a chair with only one arm free stretched out in front of him on a table.

"Where is my money cabrón? "

José said, "I don't have it."

His pleas for mercy falling on death ears as Carlos swung the machete and severed José's fingers from his right hand. José agonizing screams woke Carlos from his deep sleep. The sun was setting and he heard the familiar sounds of early evening in the Callejón; Luzmar arguing with Rodolfo, the children fighting over the play station, and the clamor of pots in Doña Ana's kitchen. He started his search for Princesa by questioning everyone in the callejon to see if anyone had seen or heard anything unusual the night before? All of the neighbors claimed ignorance and were very happy that Princesa had finally escaped the monster that was her husband. Carlos then filed a missing persons report and expanded his search to the surrounding neighborhood and community. He posted photos of his missing family and even used social media as a platform to find them. But no one had seen or heard from Princesa or the children. After several weeks, out of desperation Carlos hired a private investigator. Months and years passed and still no word of the missing family. Carlos never gave up looking for his family.

• • •

Jaime and Princesa settled into their new home located deep in the mountains Knoxville without too much difficulty. It was a lovely two bedroom ranch style house with a new nursery for the baby born six months later. On the physical plane Jaime deleted all of his social media accounts including El Brujo's website on Todos Juntos, closed all banking accounts and credit cards, and left no forwarding address

On the spiritual plane,he casted a cloaking spell to protect his family and home. It would as though El Brujo had in fact disappeared from the face of the earth. Jaime and Princesa continued to live an raised their children in Knoxville.

· · ·

It was customary practice for Jesus to call his mother Doña Carmen in Buena Vista on Christmas Eve. It was during this conversation that Jesus casually mentioned to his mother, "Can you believe that Jaime has been living here now for 20 years ?"

Several days later Doña Carmen mentioned to her neighbor Lucia that her nephew Jaime was living in the same town as her son.

Lucia said. "That is strange…he must really like it there to have stayed so long. City people usually don't like the country."

"According to Jesus, Jaime and his family are doing well there." said Doña Carmen.

The conversation of Jaime living with his family in the same town as Jesus made the rounds in the barrio. Until it reached the home of Don Bernardo, Carlos' uncle, who immediately picked up the phone to tell him. Carlos was beside himself with rage, who until now believed his family was dead. He immediately contacted the private investigator he had hired to get Jaime's exact address.

· · ·

Carlos was parked behind some trees, waiting patiently for Jaime to return home from work. Just as the investigator said, the van pulled up at exactly at 7:00 pm. The children were away at college or had moved out to live on their own. He waited a few minutes, then walk through the entrance of the house located at 601 Summit Hill. Jaime and Princesa were just sitting down at the table to have dinner when Carlos entered. Jaime stood still in s state of shock. Princesa try to scream but remained speechless in her chair, the fear paralyzing her. Even if she screamed, it did not matter because no one would hear her. The nearest house was 25 miles away.

Carlos wasted no time, he held a gun to Jaime's head, handed him a rope and said, "Tie her up or I will shoot your brains out right here, right now maricon."

It was hard for Jaime to move because panic had set in his bones but he did as he was told. Carlos worked quickly and efficiently from all his years of experience. First, he tied up Jaime to a chair. Then he covered his mouth with duct tape. Second, he checked Princesa's rope to make sure it was secured and taped her mouth shut as well. Jaime sat watching in horror as Carlos used a knife to torture Princesa in front him. Carlos left the house at about ten that night. Jesus went to the house when Jaime failed to show up to work and found the bodies three days later.

Jesus immediately dialed 911, "Please send an ambulance right away, there are two persons seriously hurt here."

When EMT arrived, Princesa was declared dead but Jaime was still alive and transported to the nearest emergency room. After being treated at the hospital, Jaime was transferred to the University Psychiatric Hospital.